DIRTY REVENGE

DIRTY SERIES BOOK 3

ELLA MILES

FREE BOOKS

EllaMiles.com/freebooks

Want to get my full-length romance *Not Sorry* for **free**?

Want to get my **free** bonus novella—*Aligned: Ever After?*

Want to know when I put my books on sale for **free or 99 cents**?

You can get all of the above and more goodies here:
EllaMiles.com/freebooks

READING ORDER

Dirty Obsession (Includes Dirty Beginning)
Dirty Addiction
Dirty Revenge

PROLOGUE

GIA

I'M the princess of darkness.

My father was the king. My brothers, princes.

I thought being a princess meant I would live in an extravagant world. Princes would be knocking at my door every day, wanting me. Or at least that's what happens in all the fairy tales. In reality, I sit locked away in the castle, and wait. Men are terrified to date me unless it assists them in doing a deal with my family. The Carini name holds too much power in this town.

I want out of the tower I've been locked away in for far too long. Dating isn't an option unless my brothers have vetted the man and deemed him worthy first. To ensure him dating me doesn't fuck with their empire. That's all they care about.

But things are changing. I'm not the girl they can lock away in the tower anymore. They can't keep me hidden from the world. I want to be free. If prince charming won't come to me, then I'm going to knock down walls to find him.

I'm a grown ass woman now. I can make my own decisions about what I want to do with my life. Just like everyone else in my family.

Father has been knocked off his thrown. He no longer belongs in this town.

Arlo is gone. He ran away with his own love, and I have a feeling he won't be back. Ever.

And Matteo, he has a new plaything he's already falling for. He may be the ruler of the Carini empire now, but soon the Carini empire will fall to love.

And when it does, where will that leave me? Alone, without even a tower to hide away in.

I apply my red lipstick and fluff my hair. I'm beautiful. I know that. I have deep olive skin, bright green eyes, and dark, flowing hair that falls down my back and stops just before the curve of my ass. I have striking features any woman would pay good money to have. My looks alone should be able to land me a handsome prince. If only I didn't have my damn name to go with it.

It's not fair. My brothers carry the Carini name with pride. As soon as a woman hears the Carini name fall from one of my brother's lips, any woman falls at his feet, worshipping him, begging him to date her, fuck her, marry her.

Not me; men hear I'm a Carini and it sends them running. Well, the good guys at least. Occasionally, there is a man who hears my name, and it makes him want me more. Because he thinks dating me will get him an in with my brothers. Those men are disgusting. They are old, gross, and twisted. They are involved in a dark world where stealing, rape, and murder are everyday occurrences.

I don't want to belong to the dark world I grew up in anymore. It served me well when I was a kid. I had a dozen rooms to myself. I never had to lift a finger to do a chore, make myself food, or go to the store for anything as simple as a tooth-brush. I got to go on the best vacations to the most exquisite places in the world. France, Bahamas, Greece, Australia, Maldives, Botswana - you name it, I've seen it all.

But now, I want my own life. I'm tired of being the dark princess. I want a normal life, with a normal boyfriend who has a normal job.

I frown, there is no way Matteo is going to let me date a normal guy with a normal job like a teacher or mechanic or something. He will say no normal guy will be able to offer me the protection I need to keep myself safe.

But maybe, normal is exactly what I need to escape this life. No one in Matteo's world is going to care about me if I'm with a boring man who makes no money. I have plenty of money saved, what would I do with more money, anyway?

Tonight, I'm going to find an ordinary man. I look down at my dark black dress, fit for Cinderella to wear to the ball. Or at least, for Cinderella's wicked stepsister. A dress like this isn't going to work to find a normal man. A dress like this will attract a prince.

I step into my closet, although 'closet' isn't the best word to describe it. It's more like a dressing room filled with all of Italy's designers' most expensive dresses. Complete with a different high heel for every occasion. I love my collection of dresses and elegant shoes. But if I keep wearing them, I'm going to remain trapped in this world. I need to change.

So I slowly slip out of the sparkly dress, until I'm standing in my black heels, stockings that attach to my garter belt, and strapless bra complete with dark embroidered roses.

What do ordinary Italian women wear when looking for a man to take them home?

My hands run over the different fabrics. Silk, lace, chiffon. So many gorgeous fabrics cut to fit my body. I stop when I get to my dark jeans.

Jeans.

I've never worn jeans out of the house. I always wear a dress or a skirt. Jeans are meant for bumming around the house. Relaxing, not gaining the attention of a man.

I grab my darkest, nicest pair. One I don't think I've ever even worn before. I slip it on and then scour my shirts. I settle on a simple black tank top with a little lace around the bust. This is the most underdressed ensemble I've ever put on. I feel wrong to be wearing something so informal.

This is what I want. I want to fit in. I want to be seen as more than a princess. No one will ever suspect me being anything but ordinary.

Now for slipping out my house unnoticed.

I walk to my bedroom and stare down at my phone lying on my dresser next to my black purse. I grab the phone to slip it into my purse, but then think better of it. Matteo can track me with my phone. I can't bring it with me.

I leave it on the nightstand, slip my purse strap over my shoulder, and strut out of my bedroom.

I walk straight to Angelo, my security team lead and prison guard, for all intensive purposes.

"I'll be ready to leave in twenty minutes."

"Of course, Miss Carini."

My lip twitches when he calls me Carini. I need to think of another name when people ask what my last name is tonight.

"First, can you fix the door lock to my bathroom? It keeps giving me problems."

"Of course, Miss Carini. I'll have it fixed and then meet you at the Lamborghini in twenty minutes."

I purse my lips. "Thank you."

I strut by him like I'm headed to the bar to fix myself a drink before I leave. Angelo thinks I'm meeting with friends at the local bar tonight. But I don't plan on doing anything typical. I plan on taking the least flashy car we own and driving it at least an hour away to the farthest, yet practical, town I can find. Then I plan on going to the busiest bar and find a man who wants me.

When Angelo enters my room, I make a hard turn to my right and head straight for the garage. I walk to the large, black Suburban. It's not mine. It is a car the security team uses to drive around on the grounds when they need to get somewhere fast. I stare at my Lamborghini that I really want to drive. It's fast, expensive, and a joy to drive. This thing is a tank that burns fuel for no reason, unlike my Lamborghini that brings fuel to life.

I can't drive the Lamborghini.

I don't want people to treat me differently. I can't show up in it.

So I climb into the tank and drive off before anyone in my family can stop me.

And for the first time in my life, I don't feel like a princess.

I don't feel like a villain.

I feel like me. A woman in seek of a man.

I smirk, staring into my rearview mirror without seeing a security team following me. *A first.*

I'm free.

———

This bar is loud, stingy, and smells like sweat. I love it.

I can't stop smiling as I slowly make my way through the crowd, trying to find the bar so I can order a drink. I've been elbowed in the face, shoved, and had my foot stepped on. Not once did anyone apologize or cower and bow after possibly hurting a Carini. No one has run away scared I'm going to have my brothers hunt them down and shoot them for hurting me.

I'm just me.

I make it to the bar, but not without some serious effort. And when I lean against the bar and raise my hand to get the bartender's attention, nothing happens.

He doesn't even glance my way over the throng of people.

"Hey, I would love to order a drink!" I holler down the long bar, which should only hold about a dozen people, but has at least three times as many crowded around it now.

I frown when nothing happens.

"Hey!" I shout again. My voice can be loud when I want it to be, but apparently, it's not enough to grab anyone's attention.

I hear a deep chuckle, and I turn to give the man my best side-eye stare.

"You don't come here often, do you?" the man asks me.

I look him up and down. He seems my age, or at least close enough. He's not dressed up at all. He's wearing jeans with holes in them, tennis shoes, and a dark grey T-shirt. He didn't even bother shaving. His dark hair covers his chin and neck, making his sparkly white teeth shine even brighter when he smiles.

I try to contain my grin. I don't want him to think I'm too anxious, but he's exactly what I'm looking for. He doesn't come from my world of fancy balls, thrown to hide the murders and evil occurring behind the scenes.

"You caught me. I'm not from this town. How do you get the bartender's attention?" I ask, giving him a tiny smile and turning entirely to face him.

His eyes drop down to my impressive cleavage. He swallows hard and shifts his legs back and forth, most likely trying to hide the jaw-dropping bulge straining in his pants.

"Like this," he pulls out a wad of cash, holds it out, and whistles loudly. The bartender turns and glides down the bar to the mysterious man who holds out the stack of twenties. The bartender takes it, pockets the large wad of cash, and then places two bottles of beer in front of us.

The man winces. "You probably aren't a beer drinker, are

you? I could get you something fancier than a beer, but it's going to take a while. All the bartender will do quickly is get you bottles of beer."

I eye the bottle and pick it up. I rarely have a beer, and never out of a bottle, always a glass. But tonight, I'm not a princess. That girl is gone. Tonight, I'm wild, adventurous, and going to go home with this man who keeps eyeing me like he wants to take me to the bathroom and fuck me.

I drink from the bottle, and the man grins like he's just won the biggest prize.

"I'm Roman Alfonso," he says.

"I'm Gia," I say, leaving off my last name intentionally.

"Well, Gia with no last name. I would love to dance with you."

I look out at the crowd of people smashed together. That doesn't look like dancing to me. They press against each other, but are barely moving anything except their hips as they grind into each other.

"Or, I could take you back to my place, and we could talk. I'd love to learn more about you somewhere where we can actually listen to each other talk," Roman says.

I'm not naive. I know what he means when he says 'talk.' He doesn't mean talk. He means fuck. And I know whatever electricity pulsing between us isn't a love attraction. *It's lust.*

But I can't ignore the way he looks at me. The way his grin softens when I return his stare. The way his hand brushes against mine, and I feel a jolt of emotion rush through me.

This may not be the man I'm going to marry, but he might be the first man I'm with who doesn't treat me like a princess. He can fuck me, leave me, and rip out my heart as any normal man would.

Roman could be the first guy who treats me like a one-night stand, instead of royalty. I want a man to help me escape my atypical world. But I could use sex with a normal guy. The last man I was with was selling weapons to Matteo. I'm tired of dangerous men.

"I live three blocks from here."

I grin and chug my beer. "Your place sounds perfect."

———

Roman's place is anything but perfect. It's tiny. It's messy. And it has a weird smell, a mix of burnt coffee and old pizza.

"You're beautiful, Gia. The most beautiful woman I've ever seen."

I roll my eyes. "How many times have you used that line?"

He chuckles. "A few times, but I've never meant it like I do right now."

His eyes twinkle when he talks. I like it.

He takes my hand and leads me toward his kitchen containing two cupboards and enough counter space to fit a single plate.

He pulls two beers out of the refrigerator and hands one to me, after popping the top off on a bottle opener stuck to the fridge.

"Thanks."

"So where are you from, beautiful?"

I narrow my eyes as I drink. "We don't have to do this. You don't care where I'm from or what I do for a living or where I went to school. You want in my pants, and that's it. So let's not pretend you are this perfect gentleman and get to the sex part."

He smirks as he leans against the counter not more than a foot from me. He cocks his head lazily to one side like he's studying me.

"What if I want more?"

My heart catches. *Stupid heart.* He doesn't want more. It's just another line.

"You don't know anything about me. How could you know if you want more or not?"

He licks his lips, and I can't stop staring. I want his lips kissing me. I want more than a kiss. I want it all with him. I want the fairy tale. I know all I'm feeling is lust. This isn't real. I don't know this man. But yet, he's perfect.

Roman reaches out and touches my flowing hair gently. "How could any man, not want you? I wasn't lying when I said you were gorgeous. You are the most beautiful fucking woman I've ever seen. I saw you from the moment you entered that bar, and I followed you. I didn't even need another drink. I was already drinking. I was dancing with a blonde bombshell, but she had nothing on you. I had to talk to you. See you. I couldn't explain it.

"You have a smart mouth. No other woman I've been with has called me a liar for saying that line."

My lips fall open as I listen to his every word.

"I'm not like most women."

He stares at me with seriousness in his eyes. "You aren't like most women. You're special."

I bite my lip, trying to control myself. But I want to throw my arms around him, kiss him, and tell him I'll marry him and have his babies all in the same breath. I don't understand what's happening. Every word he speaks is dripping with sex. His eyes are oozing with sincerity.

I know I shouldn't believe a word he is saying. It's all an act. He says this and does this with every woman he brings home to get them into bed with him. Tomorrow, he'll flip. He'll be an ass who doesn't even makes me coffee before he sends me home in a cab.

I can't stop myself though from falling instantly in love with Roman. Maybe it's the freedom he represents, but I want everything with him. I should walk away now. But I can't. My feet are cemented to the floor.

I can't move.

I can't breathe.

I can't think.

I'm lost in Roman.

"I want you Gia. So fucking badly. In my bed. As my girl-friend. As my *wife*."

My eyes shoot wide. *What the hell is he talking about?*

"I know who you are, Gia. Jeans and a tank top can't hide who you are."

Fuck.

"You're Gia Carini."

I nod.

"And I've never wanted a woman more. You're beautiful, royal, and powerful."

I bite my lip again as he grabs my neck and pulls me into a kiss. I'm lost forever as his tongue brushes against mine. I've never been kissed this hard or this passionately before. I've never been wanted. *Not for being a monster.*

Because that's what I am, a monster. I may pretend I'm a princess who hides away in a tower and has no control over my life or what my family does, but it isn't true. I have power. I could change my life if I wanted to. Stop participating in the evil my family partakes in.

I'm a Carini though. Carinis are powerful, dark creatures, incapable of real love.

Roman knows who I am. I don't know how, and I don't care. He wants me as I am. And I plan on giving him everything I have. The light, the darkness. My heart, and soul. And maybe with him, I'll find a way to be the real Gia Carini. The one I've kept hidden beneath the pretty dresses. With Roman, I can learn to love.

1

GIA

———

I sold you.

Roman's words play over and over in my head.

The light trickles in, striking my face, so all I can see is the light. I can't see the arch of the doorway overhead made of dark gray marble stone. I can't see the sharp edge of the windows next to me that open up the living room to the garden below. I can't see the beauty of the green oak trees that have been here for hundreds of years, the only things on this property entirely untouched by darkness.

All I can see is the weak shit standing in front of me. *Asshole, cunt, manwhore, gold-digger, scum of the earth, piece of shit...* Words keep coming, but they make no difference. I can call Roman whatever I want in my head, but it doesn't stop what's happening. And I won't give him the satisfaction of seeing my anger.

Roman doesn't get to see my pain. My regret. Or my anger.

He means nothing to me.

He used to be my entire world.

Now, he's nothing.

I sold you.

Roman was the one. He's sexy, charming, and despite how he dresses, he owns a string of wineries. He has money, not Carini level money, but he isn't poor. I thought he loved me. I thought I was special. I thought I was his everything.

He fucked it up once.

I thought today was about fixing his mistake.

Instead, he's fucking my life up forever.

I shield my eyes, as I see the men approaching me. I stand stoically because I know there is nothing else to do at the moment. Running is useless, I'll just end up hurt. I've seen it happen to too many women before.

I will look for an opportunity to escape once they have me, but I know that won't be more useful. In this world, there is no escaping. Even Nina and Eden didn't escape. They remained. They just changed their circumstances in their favor until this world no longer terrified them.

My only hope is that Matteo and Arlo save me. That they realize I'm gone and still have enough power in this world to save me. If they can't, I'm as good as dead.

I feel the cold, rough hands on my arms as they are jerked backward.

I sold you.

Roman's words play again.

I should focus on the men tying rope around my wrists. I need to learn as much about them as I can. Find their weaknesses. Study their faces so when I'm free, I can come back and get my revenge. But I can't focus on anyone but Roman.

Roman stands stoically as he watches the men tighten the

rope around my wrists. He seems pleased with himself. His lips curl up into a wicked grin, while his eyes deepen with a mix of lust and greed, watching me lose my freedom. He thinks he's won. But the war has only just begun. He may have won the battle, but the war is long. Carini's hold grudges, and we always get our revenge in the end.

I smirk.

"Happy to be taken? Oh, that's right. You are desperate for a man's attention. Any man. Even a demon like Dante."

Dante. That's the first time my captor has been mentioned. It doesn't ring any bells. He didn't run in our immediate circle of friends.

I continue smirking, shaking my head. "I'm not smiling. I'm smirking. You think you've won, but you forget that I'm a Carini. My days aren't numbered, but yours are."

Roman narrows his eyes at me and laughs, glancing at the men holding onto my arms. Arms that are now firmly tied behind my back. I pull at the rope, and I know there is no way my hands will break free.

"I don't think so. You are the one whose days are numbered. I'd bet good money you don't survive the week where you are going. I not only made sure to get the highest price for you, but I made sure you went to the most ruthless owner in all of Italy. Dante Russo will beat you, rape you, and kill you when he realizes how ordinary you are. You have no fight in you. Your brothers will quickly forget about you. No one will save you. And when you are dead, no one will come after me."

I search his eyes, and I find exactly what I would expect from scum like him.

"Then why is there fear in your eyes?"

Roman clears his throat and then walks toward me. "If there is any fear in my eyes, it's simply the reflection of your own."

I spit in his face.

My head whips to the side as I feel the sting of the slap against my cheek. I take a deep slow breath as the bite spreads across my cheek and to my eye.

I will not cry.

I will not show anger.

I will not show my pain.

Roman will get nothing from me.

I slowly turn my head back. I can't stop my hand from reaching instinctively to calm my cheek, which is no doubt turning redder as the seconds pass. The ropes stop me before I remember my hands are tied behind my back.

Roman's jaw spasms as he notices my hands squirming against the ropes. I know the rope is digging into my delicate skin, and will undoubtedly leave a burn in its wake, but I can't stop fighting against it. Not now that Roman has me so worked up.

He takes a step back, while the men hold me back. One of the men's hands clenches my arm so roughly the pain pulls my attention away for a second from Roman. I feel the nails digging into my flesh, and I want to cry out in pain. Tell him to stop, but I don't.

Instead, I keep all my wrath for Roman. Giving him my full attention assures him I will come after him. I will watch the whites leave his eyes as he slowly slips away from this earth to hell. Everything that happens to me from this point forward is because of Roman. And I will make him hurt for every prickle of pain I endure.

"Everything going okay in here?" a man says from behind Roman.

I force my eyes away from the snake before me and stare at the man who just entered. Clive is standing in the entryway with a cup of coffee in his hand, like this is a typical morning. Erick enters behind him, and he smirks at me.

"Yes, just about to have the garbage taken out," Roman answers.

I snarl. I can't help it. At this point, I want the men holding onto me to drag me out, so I don't have to look at Roman for another second.

Clive stands with a raised eyebrow, no doubt waiting for me to beg him to rescue me. He'll be waiting forever. I will never ask for his help. Matteo may have been willing to ask for his help to save Eden and kill my father, but I'm not willing to ask this slime for help. The cost would be too high. Matteo had to give up everything he worked for to get Eden. If I asked for Clive's help, I would merely be trading my life from Dante to Clive. I still wouldn't be free.

Roman turns from me and walks into the kitchen before returning with a stack of money. He holds it out to Clive who isn't surprised to see the money. He takes it from him eagerly.

"Thank you, Clive, for assisting me. I wasn't sure if the pull of old love would be enough to persuade Gia to come back. But I knew she couldn't resist coming back to her old home." Roman turns his head to me, and the evil oozes out of his dark eyes. "But then again, I think Gia is desperate enough that she would have come back just for a chance at my attention."

The men chuckle as if he made the funniest joke.

I hold my tongue, keeping my snark remarks to myself. Whatever I say won't help. But I will remember every word. And every bone I break on his body, every cut I inflict into his flesh, every bullet I shoot into his body will be my revenge. I will not let him live. I'm a Carini. It may take me a week, a month, or even years to escape my fate, but when I do, revenge will be sweet.

I pull on the ropes again as Roman turns away. Maybe if I can get free for a second, I can inflict some pain right now. I can't wait.

I get one arm free of the man's grasp, but the other man holding onto me jerks me back.

"Gia's feisty. She won't go easily, but it won't take long to break her. Tame her. She's already broken."

"You fucking asshole!" I yell, no longer caring what Roman thinks. I can't contain myself any longer.

Roman turns around and walks back to Clive and Erick. None of them pay me any attention as I continue to curse and yell out my threats. I will come for them all. They think my family was evil before. That Enrico was the worst, and my brothers were demons that would fight to the death. They have no idea I'm worse than all of them.

Roman, Clive, and Erick ignore me as they turn the corner and disappear into the shadows of the house. *My house.* They may occupy it now after Matteo gave it to them in exchange for their help, but I'm getting it back when I take all their lives. I'm not as forgiving as Matteo and Arlo. Clive and Erick may have little to do with me being taken, but they could have done more to prevent it. They didn't. They are just as culpable.

"Time to go, whore," the man on my left says. He has dark eyes and a scruffy beard. His biceps bulge, covered in a sleeve of tattoos. He's meant to look menacing, but he doesn't realize I've dealt with men like him my entire life. Grew up around them. His looks don't scare me. He's nothing but muscle working for his boss, Dante. He follows orders, nothing more. He won't touch me or hurt me as long as I behave.

He thinks a word like 'whore' will degrade me. Make me feel like I'm nothing. Start the process of breaking me. He doesn't realize I've been called much worse. I don't easily break, despite what Roman says.

Roman was an important lesson. One I learned far too late, but will never repeat. I will never fall in love with a man. I will never be that vulnerable again.

The other man holding my arm doesn't say anything as they start leading me to the back door of my house. This man isn't the leader. He's smaller and therefore seen as weaker. I need to wait until I'm left alone with the weaker one, then I'll make my run for it.

They don't have to pull me hard as we walk. I go willingly. Or at least that's what I make them think. Really, I'm planning in my head for when I return and slaughter all of them.

We walk out into the hot sun. Will this be the last time I see the sun? For how long? Days? Weeks? Years?

Will I be locked away in a dark dungeon? Or will I be given the freedom to walk around the house like my family always gave their slaves?

I have no way of knowing. So I lift my face up and soak in every drop of warmth. Letting the sun warm my heart and provide a memory of something positive I can take with me.

The door to the back of an SUV opens, and I'm quickly tossed into the back, just before the door is thrown shut behind me. I take a deep breath and wiggle myself up into a sitting position, recovering from falling on my face on the chilled leather seat.

Both men climb into the front without a word to each other. The car is started, and we drive off. I don't dare turn around or look in any of the side mirrors to get a last glance of my home. I refuse to let it be my last glance.

My heart beats rapidly in my chest, but other than my heart, I can't feel anything. Not fear or pain. Nothing.

But they made their first mistake. They tied my hands together, but not my legs. They sit in the front and not the back. They don't think I will run. They believe I'm already broken as Roman said. That I've relented to being someone's slut already.

I try to keep my lips thin, my expression blank, as if I'm in shock. It doesn't matter though, because the men in front pay me no attention. They think there is no way for me to escape. They're wrong.

2

CASPIAN

I LIFT the cup of coffee to my lips, scanning for any signs of Dante Russo or his men. I spot one man at the bar, out of the corner of my eye. Another member of his security team strolls down the quaint, brick sidewalk that has been here for hundreds of years.

I shake my head. Dante's men stand out like a sore thumb. They need to learn to at least wear clothing that helps them to blend in. Look inconspicuous. Otherwise, they might as well stand at Dante's side and look as menacing as possible to try to keep people away.

"Mr. Conti, a pleasure to meet you. I've heard many great things about you. Although, I'm surprised to learn you didn't bring a security team with you since that's what you specialize in," Dante says, towering over me at my table.

I resist the urge to roll my eyes at this man. I simply stand and hold out a hand. "Just because your men haven't identified my security team, doesn't mean I don't have one."

"Touché, Mr. Conti," Dante says, as we both sit back down.

He scans me up and down, and I wait for the comment about my age.

"You seem young to have become such a leading voice in security, Mr. Conti."

Yep, there it is. I do roll my eyes this time. I'm sick of men like him thinking because I'm young, and I didn't inherit my company from my father like he did, that I'm not capable.

"Why did you take this meeting with me, Dante, if you didn't think I was capable of delivering?" My eyes burn into his as I speak. I hate men who waste my time.

"I never said you were incapable, just young, Mr. Conti." He repeats my formal name. He wants me to give him the same respect, but he hasn't earned it. Dante Russo may be a powerful man, but that doesn't mean I'm willing to cower at his feet like everyone else in this country. I may not have his money, but everything I earned, I built on my own. I was given nothing.

I take another sip of my coffee while I wait for him to speak again. I'm anxious, too anxious. And if I let him know that, he will realize this is more than just a deal for me. So much more. Dante doesn't understand I know exactly who he is.

"As I said, I've heard many great things from you, Mr. Conti. And as you know, security and discretion are of utmost importance to me. Money isn't an issue. I will pay you well, if you are, in fact, the best."

I don't care about his money. But I don't tell him that. It's time to impress. "You have two men at the bar. One on the street. Four in cars around the perimeter. And one sniper on the building across the street. They all use a Retevis RT21 system to communicate with, which can easily be dismantled..." I pull out the device from my pocket and press the button. "With the touch of a button."

Dante scans his men, all grabbing for the earpieces in response to the loud fog sound blowing out their eardrums.

I nod at my sister behind me, and my team moves in on all of his men. His men drop to the ground, put there by my team. My team knows how to blend into the shadows.

Dante freezes as a gun presses against his temple, but only after his gun in the back of his pants is pulled free and tossed to the side.

I smirk as I lean back in my chair, and Dante glares at me. "Meet my sister, Mr. Russo," I say, using his last name to make a greater impact.

Dante lets out a breath and chuckles.

I nod to Adela who slowly lowers her gun.

"I'm impressed. I didn't realize your team was here, or that you had a sister." Dante eyes Adela with lust. This is why I never tell anyone I have a sister. She is fully capable of taking care of herself, but I can't handle creeps staring at her like a piece of meat.

"That's all, Adela," I say.

She nods and disappears again.

"Like I told you when I contacted you last week, I'm the best. I believe in being discreet and working with the best technology around. Technology that no one but me owns."

"How long to get your systems and my team up to your level?"

"I can have my system installed in your home as soon as payment hits my bank account. A week. Shorter, if you prefer. And your team? I would recommend firing them and starting over. If I hire your team, I can have you the perfect team within two weeks."

Dante frowns. "My men are good men. They have been with me for a long time. I trust them."

I glance over at the man slowly dusting himself off after my team tackled him to the ground. "Ezio there? He's been stealing money, drugs, jewels, anything he thinks he can take from you without you noticing for years."

I glance toward the man at the bar. "Gareth has been getting paid by Domenèc for any interesting tidbits about you. Do I need to continue?"

"No."

"Would you like me to find you a better-qualified team and fire your current team?"

"Yes, hire me the best you can find. No women, though."

I snigger. I wouldn't expect anything less from a chauvinist like him.

"It's not good for the business I run. Women bodyguards are too emotional to handle the work I require."

I nod. I don't doubt women get too emotional when they realize he smuggles women like drugs. Although, I bet most women, if they worked with Dante, wouldn't say anything. They'd be too afraid they might face the same fate if they told anyone.

"No women. Got it."

Dante scowls as he looks at his men with his hands folded on the table like this is a simple business meeting, and we aren't talking about men's lives. "No need to fire them. I'll take care of it."

A chill creeps down my spine at his words. I know how he will 'handle it.' They will all be dead by morning. Not that they don't deserve it, or that I disagree with his tactics. I would do the same if he left the firing to me.

His phone buzzes, and he pulls it out. "One moment, Mr. Conti. I need to take this. Then, we can discuss your price."

I nod as he stands, leaving me alone at the small table on the edge of the sidewalk. I sip more of my coffee as a black Escalade pulls up outside. The man in the driver's seat rolls down his window as he speaks with the man on the sidewalk.

I narrow my eyes. These men aren't part of Dante's security team. They do other work for him. I don't have time to deduce precisely what work, before the back door is thrust open and a beautiful woman falls to the stone drive.

I can't take my eyes off of her as she pulls herself to a standing position. Her arms are tied behind her back, and I have no doubt what she was doing in the back of the SUV or who she belongs to. She's one of Dante's women. He hasn't touched her yet, that much is clear. She has fight and determination in her piercing green eyes, visible even though we are several feet apart.

Her eyes shine brightly beneath her black hair that cascades down the sides of her face. When my eyes find her breasts, I bite my lip and groan. Perfectly round mounds spill out over the top of her shirt. And I don't even dare let my eyes travel down her long, lean legs or heels I want digging into my back as my cock slams inside her.

I don't know who this woman is. But I will. My cock aches at the sight of her. I have to have her. I have to know her. Go near her. Touch her. Taste her. Fuck her.

It's clear from her designer outfit and the way she holds her head high that she comes from money. Old wealth, no doubt. I don't know how Dante got her. Is she payment for an old debt? Did he steal her?

I would understand the urge if he stole her. I'm very much feeling the same, and I've only just seen her.

The dark beauty considers her next move. I see it in her eyes. She wants to run. Is desperate to. But she glances down at her spiky heels and the men who are slowly becoming aware she is no longer in the back of the car. *Amateurs.* How hard is it to keep a woman retained in a car? It's clear the ropes will do nothing to contain a fire like her.

Her eyes search quickly for any chance at escape. For freedom. For help.

Her eyes stop when they find mine. For a flicker of a second,

I think I see lust in her eyes as she checks me out. But realize it is most likely my own lust reflected in her eyes. No woman in her predicament would think about such silly things as lust at a moment like this.

She runs toward me. She's choosing *me*. Thinking I'll be her salvation.

She's wrong.

She may think she sees some kindness in my blue eyes, but there isn't any caring left. Any kindness I once had was taken from me years ago, as easily as her freedom is being ripped from her now.

She stumbles, approaching me. My arms go out automatically, catching her as she falls into my aching lap.

She smiles, catching her breath. She thinks she's safe in my arms.

I smirk. *She couldn't be more unsafe.*

"Help. Please."

I raise an eyebrow as I get a whiff of her shampoo and perfume. It's strong, just like her. But not overwhelming. Just strong enough. Not overly flowery, but feminine nonetheless.

I stroke her hair, resisting my urge to grab the long strands roughly and drag her to my car waiting on the next block so I can fuck her in my bed.

What the hell?

I shouldn't want to fuck her. She's Dante's. Fucking her would ruin everything I've planned and worked on for years.

I push her up until she's standing again. Hoping that some distance between us will ease my discomfort and need for her. My cock only strains harder in my jeans.

Jesus, she's gorgeous.

Her eyes widen. She thinks I was helping her when I helped her stand. She believes that was kindness. She may be strong, but she has no idea how to read people. She needs to learn fast if she's going to survive a year with Dante.

"Help me. Please. A man named Dante has kidnapped me."

She glances behind her and sees the guards approaching. I think she's going to change her mind and make a run for it. It's instinct. Any person would run.

But not her.

She keeps her feet firmly planted, as if she knows exactly what's coming and is ready to face it. She does everything she can to show no fear. Her body stands tall, robust. Her body doesn't quiver or shake. Her breathing is steady and calm. Her lips are pulled back into a thin line. Even her eyes do everything possible to hide any fear.

I read people for a living though. So I know, despite how calm she appears on the outside, her pulse is racing. I grab her wrist.

She smiles a tiny bit, thinking I'm offering to help her.

I feel her pulse racing fast. It's one of the signs she can't hide. No matter how tough she tries to act on the outside.

"Help. They are going to take me. Call my brothers. They will help me. I'm Gia Ca—"

Her voice is cut off by Dante's. "You've stopped my new whore from escaping, Mr. Conti. You are well worth your asking price."

I take Gia's hand and hand her over to Dante.

Gia. It's a beautiful name that fits her well.

Her eyes widen when she realizes she fell into the lap of the devil instead of a saint. She wasted her one chance of escape on me.

She swallows hard, trying to keep her calm facade, when Dante pulls her into his body. He takes a deep breath, letting her know he smells her, unlike when I tried to hide my desire to smell her.

Dante grabs her chin and forces her to look up at him. He licks his lip like he can't wait to get her back to his house.

My insides burn, seeing her in his arms. She's mine. I found her first.

"I think I underpaid for you, whore. You are trying to hide it from me. But you are most definitely a spitfire I will get the pleasure of breaking. I look forward to it. Not many women would attempt to break free this quickly. Most are in too much of shock to even react."

"Go to hell," she says.

He grins, tightening his grip on her. But she doesn't react, other than a glare.

Dante turns to me. "As you can see, I have some things to attend to. I'll have the money to you by the end of the day. Call my secretary to discuss when you can set up my new system. Maybe I'll even let you play with my new toy?" Dante licks her face, and she shudders.

I growl, but it's so low I'm not sure either of them heard me.

Dante is too focused on Gia. He grips her tightly as he walks her to the waiting Escalade, where his incompetent men wait. He shoves her in the back and, I have no doubt, will be climbing in, right next to her, to ensure she doesn't attempt an escape again.

Gia looks at me one last time. I was her only hope, and now that hope is gone. But I don't see that reflected in her eyes. Instead, I see fire. She studies me, and I know I've just been added to her list. She wants revenge, to make me suffer like she is going to suffer.

I can't take my eyes off her until the door is shut, blocking my view with the tinted windows. Even then, I don't stop watching until the SUV drives away.

Gia wants her revenge on me for not helping her. For turning her over to a barbarian. I do not doubt she will one day get her revenge. But if I'm going to be punished by her, I'm going to do something worth getting punished for.

Dante invited me to his house to share her. I don't share, but I can't stay away. I'll fuck her, get her out of my system, so I can forget about her and return to my own revenge. While I happily wait for the day she carries out hers. It will be worth it, if only to see her piercing eyes again.

3
____

GIA

MR. CONTI.

That's the name of the man I put my faith in. I don't even know his first name. But I risked my only hope of escape on him. I thought he would go to the police. Call my brothers. Figure out who I am and realize the reward my brothers would give him would be more than generous. Instead, I'm pinned in the back of the SUV with Dante and his men.

I thought I saw kindness in Mr. Conti's eyes when I stepped out of the SUV. I knew I couldn't outrun the idiots who drove me. My guards may not have much of a brain between their ears, but they are built. All muscle. I couldn't outrun them with my hands tied behind my back and my high heeled shoes, so I chose a man; a man with tired, gray eyes and what I thought might be warmth hiding behind those eyes.

I was wrong.

Whatever I saw, it wasn't kindness. Mr. Conti is friends with the devil.

I made the worst mistake I could. I trusted a stranger because I thought I could sense something more than cold indifference oozing off of him.

Mr. Conti turned me over to Dante without a second thought. I am nothing to him. Not even a woman, just another way for Mr. Conti to show his loyalties to Dante.

I swallow down my regret, trying not to think too hard about the gorgeous man sitting back at the quaint coffee shop I've been to hundreds of times before. Amante. I love the place. I never realized monsters hung out there.

Beautiful, handsome, dark beasts. Mr. Conti may be evil, but if I were free, he would have been precisely the type of man I went after. Tall, muscular, wealthy, and hiding a dark past beneath his grimace. When his eyes soaked into me, full of want and desire, I saw the hunger in his eyes. I even let myself feel it for one second. One full second, and then I stopped myself.

It might have been the last time a man looked at me with a hint of lust where I had a choice in what happened afterward. From now on, if any man looks at me that way, I won't have a choice to say no. They will take whatever they want from me.

Mr. Conti was supposed to be my savior. But he won't help me.

My brothers don't have a clue I'm missing. And by the time they figure out I'm gone, it will be too late.

I have to save myself.

Dante grabs my chin and forces me to look at him again.

"Such a beauty."

I growl and jerk my head out of his grasp.

He grabs my chin and pulls me so close to his face I can smell his breath; a disgusting mix of coffee, cigarettes, and rotting flesh.

I glare at him as I lean away from him.

"I will enjoy breaking you, whore."

"My name is Gia," I say, although I don't know if he used my name if I would feel any better. Gia feels more personal. But it's better than 'whore.'

Dante cocks his head to the side and glances up at the man in the passenger seat, perplexed, as if to say, "Can you believe this?"

"I've never had a woman quite like you. Usually, the women I take are in too much shock to say anything, especially nothing that snarky."

"That wasn't snarky. You haven't seen me be snarky yet."

"I don't doubt that. I will enjoy slowly snuffing the fire out of you as the days pass. Usually, I need a new woman within a week. None of my previous conquests have lasted long, and I'm not into necrophilia. I once had a woman last a month. She had a man she was living for, fighting for. You don't have a man you are fighting to get back to, do you, whore?"

I don't react when he calls me a whore. It's just a word. I need to prepare myself for much worse.

"No, I don't need a man. When I escape, I will be returning with an army to kill every single one of you. But don't worry, I'll kill you last, slowly, for payback for everything you do to me."

His eyes blaze, and his nostrils steam. I've just turned him on.

Shit.

"So you have relented I will have my way with you then, whore?"

"No."

He strokes my hair slowly and gently, before grabbing my hair forcefully, jerking my head back as his lips hover over my ear.

"I will have my way with you, whore. Lucky for you, I don't have any clients to see this week. So you and I will have an entire week to get to know each other. And you can wish you had a man in your life who might rescue you, or at least to cloud your memories when I fuck you."

I suck in a breath. I hate how his hot breath breathes down

my neck. My body freezes, hoping he will stop. But I need to fight my urge to stop moving. Not fighting back won't get me anywhere. I need to fight to get free. Even if it means I might get more injuries until I finally break free.

Dante jerks me away from his mouth so he can look me in the eyes.

"I think you are going to be my greatest conquest of all, whore." Dante turns his attention to his men in the front seat who have largely ignored our conversation. "How long do you think my new whore will survive?"

"You are the greatest master, sir. You will tame her within the week, and then how long she survives will be up to you."

"Two weeks, sir."

Dante licks his bottom lip slowly as he turns back to me.

I squirm back against the door, trying to get as far away from him as possible.

"I'm feeling generous. I'll give you two months. I think you are stronger than the rest. You have spirit and fight, and you fight all for yourself, not for the love of a man. I admire that, whore. But in the end, it won't help you. You're mine now. The sooner you learn to behave, the sooner this will all end."

End.

He means this will only end when I die.

I may have made some mistakes in choosing my escape, but this will not end with my death. Even if I do die, Arlo and Matteo will never stop until Dante is dead. They will get my revenge. He underestimates the Carini bloodline if he thinks he will survive this.

I don't say any of that to him. It won't help. For now, I need to prepare myself for what's next. Good thing I've had years of practice.

The car slows, and I stare up with wide eyes at the house

which, I assume, will soon become my prison. It's a large house, almost as big as the Carini mansion, but unlike the warm, ancient, and inviting Carini mansion, this house feels cold and indifferent. The building has high, light-gray brick walls. The front door is a dark wood that looks like it's meant on a dungeon cell, not the front door of a home. But then again, this isn't a home; it's a prison.

I swallow and feel my heart beating rapidly. Maybe I'll die of a heart attack before I even get inside. That would be the easy way out. No suffering.

I'm used to suffering; I remind myself.

Whatever Dante has planned for me, I can survive. I always survive.

I don't realize the men are already out of the car until my door is thrust open, and I almost fall to the concrete ground below.

A burst of thunder sends a jolt through me, almost as if restarting my heart. I take a deep breath, and I feel stronger than I've felt in a long time. My heart rate slows to a much steadier pace.

I'm a Carini. There is nothing I can't face.

I step out of the car as hands clasp around my bicep again. I won't be forced into the house. I won't be dragged. I will walk in proudly like I own the place. I'm different than his other whores. And therefore, I have an advantage. I can't change and start acting scared.

Raindrops pour down as I walk the few feet to the front door. I feel every drop. I love the rain, but today the rain mirrors my mood. Thunder rolls again, but this time I don't jump. It sounds more like a chorus beating loudly in the background, reminding me I have someone on my side. I'm as strong as the thunderous sound.

Dante opens the door, and I step in with one of his men still gripping my arm. I quickly scan everything in sight. I need information if I'm going to survive. I need to know every exit. Every security camera. Every guard. I need to know every person in this house. Every car. Every weapon. Only then will I be able to escape.

"You never cease to surprise me, whore," Dante says as he takes over for his guard, whom he quickly dismisses.

I raise an eyebrow. It's just him and me.

He either thinks he can easily overpower me. Control me. Or he has more security guards waiting to take me out if I run.

Dante isn't stupid, unlike his men.

He won't leave himself vulnerable. He wants me too badly to give me a chance to escape. He's testing me. Seeing if I will run so he can punish me.

Think differently.

My instinct is to run, but that's not what I need to do. He wants me because I'm a spitfire, and he would enjoy breaking me.

I won't let him win.

I need to be different.

I need to pretend I'm into him. That I want him to fuck me. That I've been so desperate for male attention, I'd even fuck a man like him. It's going to suck, but it might be the only way for freedom. I can pretend. That's all this is, pretend.

I took acting classes in high school. I was good. I can do this.

"You have a beautiful home, Mr. Russo."

He raises an eyebrow.

"Thank you, whore. It doesn't have the views you are used to, but then again, you haven't lived in a home like this for several weeks now. I'm sure you are aching to know what it feels like again."

He strokes my face, and I do everything I can to not react negatively to his touch. I don't miss the double meaning of his words. He doesn't think a man has touched me in weeks. He's right. I need to let him know just how right he is.

"I'm looking forward to it," I say, my eyes meeting his, challenging him to call me out on my words.

He smirks, pleased with my response.

So I continue. "You're right. I haven't been with a man in months. I thought Roman was the one. I thought he loved me and wanted me. I was wrong. Roman is half the man you are."

Dante doesn't respond. His eyes deepen though at my words. He grabs my wrists, bound with rope behind my back. He spins me until my back is to him.

I resist the urge to glance back at him. I need to show him I trust him with my body.

So instead, I focus on studying my surroundings, but it's impossible with him breathing down the back of my neck again.

I feel something sharp and cold against my wrists.

Shit.

He's going to cut me. I should never have turned my back to him.

My breath catches as he cuts the rope from my wrists. My hands pull apart, and I rub them gingerly, examining the red bumps and abrasions which have formed a perfect circle where the rope used to be.

I turn slowly, trying to show appreciation in my eyes, as I look at Dante.

"Thank you."

He stowes the knife in his back pocket. I try not to look too eager to know where he hides a weapon. As much as I want to go over to him now and steal the knife, I won't. It would be easy enough to distract him with a kiss while retrieving it from his pocket. I resist. It won't get me anywhere. Even if I killed him, his men would attack me. I would never get out alive. And if I missed, I would have to deal with his wrath. I would have played my cards too early.

No, I need to wait. Have patience. Get him to trust me and let his guard down.

"This way, whore," he says, snapping his fingers.

I follow, still getting used to having my hands free again. When I catch up to him, I hook one of my hands around his arm.

His lips curl up a little, but otherwise, he doesn't react. I'm used to hanging onto men I don't have feelings for. I've played the interested, hot woman too many times for my father or brothers. I know how to distract men.

And I do just that as Dante leads me around his house, showing off various pieces of art or views he thinks are impressive. They aren't. Nothing in this house is remarkable.

"I have one more room to show you. I think it will be your favorite," he says, his voice deeper than it's been.

I know what room he is talking about. *A bedroom.* I know what's coming. Dante isn't a patient man. He wants what he paid for. He wants to fuck me. This is the moment that will define our relationship. I need to jump on him, seem needy and wanting before he has a chance to rape me. I need to be the one to initiate the sex. Even if it destroys me to pretend.

We walk down a long hallway, and I try to pretend I'm walking down a hallway in the Carini mansion. I try to think of my niece. How beautiful she is. I need to fight to get back to her. She deserves to have me as an aunt who will spoil her and take her shopping.

But even thoughts of the most precious creature on the planet can't hold my attention when he opens the door to the room at the end of the hallway.

It's not a bedroom.

Well, there is a bed in the room, but I wouldn't call it a bedroom. It's a torture chamber.

Whips line the walls. Ropes, chains, handcuffs. Poles topped with metal hoops stand throughout the room, for restraints to be tied to. Walking around the room, inspecting the equipment, I stop when I get to sharper, bloody devices. Blood from other women tortured in this room. I can't think about this.

Dante is darker than I ever imagined. He has a twisted soul. Fucking him won't be enough to save me. I have to be willing to let him beat and torture me.

I turn back to Dante, with a wicked smile on my face, and walk calmly toward him.

I wrap my arms around his neck, and he raises an eyebrow while staring down at me. His eyes are burning with dark desire.

I run my thumb over his bottom lip. "You're into BDSM. Good thing, I'm the queen of BDSM."

This goes well beyond a healthy BDSM relationship. This is a sick fetish. Even if he was doing these things to women consensually, there is something very wrong with a man that wants to torture a woman this badly.

I continue my plan though, keeping my breathing and heart steady as I raise my lips to his and kiss him.

I try to keep pleasant thoughts in my head so that he won't sense my disgust.

Mr. Conti pops into my head. He's a good-looking man. He's a fiend, but better looking than Dante.

I pretend I'm kissing Conti. I drop the mister from my head because it seems too formal. Conti kisses me harder, sweeping his tongue into my mouth, letting me know how much he needs to be in control of my body.

I can't hold the image long in my head, and slowly I pull away when Dante returns to my vision. I keep my hand on his neck, trying my best to show affection. I bite my lip and watch his eyes burn into my lip.

"I must admit, this is a fantasy of mine. Being taken by a handsome man like you. Tortured, fucked, like only a man like you can fuck. I want this. Tell me what you want me to do, and I'll do it, master."

Dante grabs my wrist, and I think he's going to give in to my words and body. His eyes and cock pressing hard into my stomach say as much.

I smile seductively. Trying to force him to give into his desire for me instead of the darker, controlling side.

Before I realize what's happening, I'm thrown hard into the wall behind me, and I crumple to the floor.

My head is pounding, and I feel the blood oozing down my back.

I don't know what I hit my head on, but it was hard and sharp.

Dante takes his time strutting over to me. He has more patience than I thought.

"Stand up, whore."

I don't know how he expects me to stand. I can barely see. He's merely a haze of a shadow in front of me.

I try to scramble to my feet, but the dizziness drops me back on my ass, and I hit my head again.

"I said, stand," he commands.

I try, but it's an impossible task.

He grabs my wrist, jerking me to my feet, and I swear I feel bones cracking in my wrist.

"I don't play games with my whores. You aren't my first. I've had hundreds, and I know every game in the book. You will not win. I will destroy you."

I nod because I think it's what he wants, and I can't take

another hit. I know I have a concussion. Possibly a broken skull or wrist. I can't think straight. I can't see. I'm not even sure if I exist, or if any of this is real.

I'm either dead or about to be raped. And I pray I'm already dead. Either way, I'm in hell.

4

GIA

Days. Weeks. Months.

I have no idea how much time has passed since Dante stole me.

Time means nothing anymore.

I thought I was a force to be reckoned with. I thought I would fight every second of every day for my freedom. Dante taught me how mistaken I was.

Most seconds I can't even lift my head up off the ground. I can't stand. I can't see.

Seconds are how I measure my life. I can't think beyond that.

This second, I'm lying on the cold floor of the torture room. I haven't left since I arrived. There are no windows. No bathroom. No light.

It's a dark room, but I welcome the pitch-black. It helps me sleep at all hours of the day, which is the only reason I'm still breathing.

Sleep has been my savior.

I hear footsteps outside my door. Dante said he had a surprise in store for me when he returned. Was that hours, or days, ago?

Dante's surprises aren't surprises. He's given me half a dozen surprises already, and they all involved bringing in more men to share in the 'fun,' as he calls it.

Dante talks like he hasn't broken me yet. Like I still have a fighting spirit he hasn't figure out how to tame yet.

He's wrong. I'm broken. Physically I know I have dozens of broken bones. My left wrist flops when Dante ties me up, my right knee shattered when Dante whacked me with a bat. I'm not sure I have any ribs left intact after Dante kicked me numerous times in the chest.

I have nothing left to fight for.

Even if I did survive, I would be a hollow shell compared to the woman I was before. I would go through my days staring into the abyss, my mind most definitely stuck in the dungeon my body is trapped in now.

Yes, occasionally I gather enough strength to spit in some-one's face, bite a finger, or give a swift kick to a groin, if I'm really in a fighting mood. But it's not fighting. It's *revenge*.

I don't care if I die anymore. I just need Dante and Roman to suffer.

The door crashes open, rattling the doorframe, as steady boots stomp inside my cage.

I used to shutter at such sounds, but I no longer do. I don't care if Dante is here or if he's gone. It makes no difference. I no longer feel pain. I feel nothing.

Lights flick on, and I close my eyes. The light too bright for me to keep my swollen eyes open.

"Such a good whore. You are exactly where I left you."

I don't answer. Where did Dante expect me to go? I have a broken leg, and he tied my legs with shackles to the post behind me. I didn't have any options but to stay exactly where he left me: naked and slumped on the floor.

"Stand, whore."

I can't stand, idiot.

I feel Dante's eyes burning into me. I expect the kick will come soon, but I don't brace myself for it.

"No," I spit back. Maybe I'm feeling more defiant than I realized.

The kick jerks my body backward and hard against a wall. Other than my body moving, I don't feel the pain I would expect from being kicked with solid boots at full force. It's all the same pain to me.

It benefits me. I no longer whimper or groan. I give Dante none of the sounds that turn him on. Now, he tries harder to evoke those sounds from me. He'll keep attempting until I'm dead.

Maybe today will be that day?

No.

That word has hovered around in my head and heart every time I've wished I was dead.

No.

I don't know why. I don't know where the hope or strength comes from, but it floats through my body, filling my soul, all the same.

No.

"Stand, whore."

"No."

"I told you she had a spirit, unlike any woman I've ever had. She's been here a month, and she never breaks. In fact, she may have grown stronger. She controls her whimpers for the most part, but today, I think that will change."

Another kick to the ribs. This one doesn't send me flying back. I'm already against the wall. I hear something cracking in my body. What was it this time? More ribs? My leg? Or my skull cracking?

No. No. No. Don't focus on the tiny slivers of pain creeping in.

I'm dead. Nothing can hurt me.

I feel the tears starting in my eyes. I don't know how they formed. I'm dehydrated from crying so much when I first got here. I thought all my tears were empty.

One month, Dante said. Have I really been here that long?

It seems like longer and shorter at the same time.

One month. Has Matteo or Arlo realized I'm gone yet? I told Matteo I would be gone for a month. After not hearing from me, or my security team, for this long, would he come for me finally? How much longer do I have to hold on?

Another kick.

A low growl.

Wait...a growl? Did I make that sound?

My puffy eyes flicker open, as wide as I can bring them. I don't have access to a mirror, but I don't doubt I look bad. My face has to be all sorts of shades of reds, blacks, and yellows, as different parts of my face are in different phases of healing. And my cheeks, in particular, are at least twice the size they usually are.

I see men. At least five standing over me. I don't bother to count the exact number. That should scare me. It doesn't.

One more kick.

And this time I definitely hear the growl. It's not mine. My head darts in the direction of the sound. My eyes are too clouded to see clearly, but I swear I see an angel.

"Mr. Conti, would you like a turn?" Dante says, lust dripping off his voice.

Mr. Conti. A vision creeps in, one I've played over and over in my head. Mr. Conti barges into the dungeon with my brothers. He apologizes profusely, telling me he never wanted to turn me over to Dante. He had to, to save me later. But now that Conti's here, standing over me, I realize it was a stupid dream that will never become a reality.

Mr. Conti moves forward, and he still looks like an angel in my eyes. A cloud of fog forms around his head, shining brightly in the darkness of the world I'm trapped in. I know it's just my eyes playing tricks on me, but he was the culprit. He was the one who growled. He didn't like what Dante was doing to me. This man won't hurt me. I don't care why he's here; he won't hurt me.

A sly grin forms on Conti's face, and it warms me a second.

Then I'm kicked. Hard into the wall.

And the illusion of Conti being an ally shatters. He's as much of a monster as any man in this room.

"Now stand, whore," Dante says.

"Don't you think if I could stand, I would? I want nothing more than to look you all in the eyes so that when I do get free, I will know who to torture and kill."

Men chuckle. Not Conti. His eyes never leave mine. His jaw twitches and I swear his eyes are trying to tell me something, but I have no idea what.

He's not on my side. No one is. It's just my imagination.

Dante snaps his fingers, and I'm on my feet. Hands grip my arms too tightly, and I try to balance on my uninjured leg only to realize it's just as useless as my other leg. *When did Dante break my other leg? How did I miss that?*

"Oh whore, today I share you, but tonight, you're mine alone," Dante says in my ear before biting my earlobe.

He's never gentle. Not even for a second. He's relentless in his pursuit to cause me harm. It never stops. I don't know how he has the energy to hurt me while still keeping up with his job.

"On the bed," Dante orders.

Hands drag me to the bed. Shackles release from my legs. No longer needed with five powerful men in the room. Not that it was needed before. I couldn't walk, but I guess Dante thought I would crawl.

I'm spread open, something that used to embarrass me now seems like nothing.

Look at my body you disgusting cunts! Look at what a beautiful woman you are breaking, and tell me how you would like your karma handed to you for what you've done. The words form in my head, but I don't think I have the strength to make them leave my mouth.

"The guest of honor can have his way with her first," Dante says.

I don't care who the guest of honor is. They will all rape me. Defile me. Break me.

No.

I won't let them break me.

Conti moves in close, settling between my legs, grabbing them with his hands. He's going to be the first to rape me. I pull hard once. It's all the energy I have. One of my legs gets free, and I kick Conti in the side. He doesn't move. It was a weak kick. I'm surprised I even had the strength.

The grips on my arms and legs tighten as I'm spread wider for him. His clothes are still on, but the men don't usually reveal anything but their cock to me. While I'm naked. Always.

I watch as Conti begins to undo his pants and a single tear trickles down my cheek. I hate the damn tear. And I don't even have arms to wipe it away. Every man here can see my weakness.

It's been a long time since I cried. Or felt anything. But watching as my angel turns back into the devil has done it.

I close my eyes tightly. I won't open them again. I need to find a happy place to survive. But there is no memory or dream left which can take me away from here. I need to sleep. But I can't.

I open my eyes again. I can't help myself. I need to see Conti turn into the monster I knew he always was. I need to make sure he's added firmly to my revenge list, instead of living in my fantasies.

Smack. A hand shoots fire against my face. One of the hardest assaults I've ever experienced. My head is spinning, and I can't open my eyes.

Conti punched me in the face. He's too much of a coward to rape me fully conscious. *Asshole.*

I start drifting in and out of consciousness, but I won't fully let sleep consume me. I'll remember every moment of this, while I play brutal images of what I will do to Conti when I get free. He's a bigger monster than all the rest. And now I know I'm really on my own.

5

CASPIAN

"LEAVE," *I say.*

The men in the room stutter, not sure what to do as they look to Dante to give them orders.

"Leave!" I shout.

The men let go of Gia's hands and legs and leave the dark room. Dante is the last to leave, but he doesn't say anything as he eventually leaves me alone with Gia.

I rest between her stretched legs that are no doubt broken, but it doesn't stop me from pushing her wider.

She moans.

I lean down and kiss her lips. Lips I've been desperate to taste since she fell into my lap weeks ago.

Her lips are soft and delicious, but it's not what I want. I want her to kiss me back.

I lower my lips tasting her neck, breasts, and stomach.

And then I pull my rock hard cock out of my pants. I shouldn't do this. I shouldn't fuck her, but I can't stop myself.

I'm desperate for her.

She's all I've thought about for the last four weeks. I almost did something incredibly stupid. I wanted to steal her from Dante before he touched her, but it would have fucked up all my plans. So I didn't. I let him touch her.

I growl.

That was a mistake I won't repeat. She's mine.

I'm not a better man than Dante. In fact, I might be worse. I let an innocent woman suffer when I could have done something to stop it, but I chose not to.

"Gia Carini, you will be mine. You don't belong to Dante. You belong to me."

She whimpers.

She hates me, just as she does Dante. And I deserve her wrath.

I should stop, but I have to have a taste of her. I have to fuck her. I can't stop myself.

My cock sinks into her slit; wet and welcoming. I don't know what she's dreaming about, but it's dirty if her cunt is this slick for me. I sure didn't do anything to turn her on.

Beautiful.

The most beautiful, fierce woman on the planet lies beneath me, encircling my cock. I should stop. But I can't. Dante didn't break her, but I can. First, I'll steal her; then I'll destroy her.

I walk up the stairs to the front door with my team encircling the house. My sister and second best, Terence, stand behind me.

Today, everything changes. Dante's team will be taken out and replaced by a team I hired for him. Dante wanted to do all the killing himself, but he realized he couldn't. So instead, he took out his most valuable men in the darkness of last night. Today, everyone else dies in the daylight.

Then, my first phase will be complete. I'll be able to monitor everything he does and be able to make my move on Dante whenever I want. Once I confirm what I already know about Dante.

And then I can steal Gia.

No.

I can't steal her. It will ruin everything.

But I have to have her.

My inner conflict never stops. Not since I had her in my grasp.

Today, I need to focus on my job. I'll decide what to do about Gia tomorrow.

I knock on the door and am surprised when Dante opens the door. I expected one of his guards. Did he jump the gun and take out all his men himself? I do not doubt Dante is capable enough of doing the job. It doesn't matter to me. Killing demons like Dante's men pleases me. I'll admit it. But I'm just as happy to have someone else do the bloodshed, as long the task is done.

"Mr. Conti, come in," Dante says, not giving anything away.

I see his men out of the corner of my eye. Dante told them I was here to work on the security system I installed a few weeks ago. It's a lie. My security system is running flawlessly. Right now, it's allowing my team to know the precise location of Dante's men, so they can all be taken out at the same moment.

I follow Dante into the living room with Terence and Adela following behind me.

I freeze at the entrance when I see Gia. I wasn't expecting her. It is clear from the security tapes that Dante never allows her to leave the room she was locked in. But today, she's lying on the black leather couch. A rope is tied around her hands and legs. She's naked and bruised, but not broken. I'm not sure if anything can truly break her.

I can.

I don't know why Gia is here, but she's going to distract me, and most likely Dante, from doing the job.

"Want to put your whore away before we get to work?" I ask Dante, not liking using the word 'whore' to describe Gia. She is anything but a whore. *Warrior, gorgeous, precious, angel.* All those words describe her so much better.

Dante laughs. "Don't worry. She won't distract us from our job. I want her to watch."

My lips thin, but otherwise I don't give away my disgust. Dante wants Gia to watch, in an attempt to break her. If she sees the carnage, it might scare her. Death has a way of doing that to people.

I suspect Gia isn't one of those people. For one, she seems completely prepared for her own death. And two, she's a Carini. My understanding about Carinis is they are as ruthless as Dante. She may not have killed anyone with her own hands, but she's seen death before.

And she won't care if men, who have held her captive, die. In fact, she will rejoice at the sight.

I nod and glance at my ready sister behind me. I stare at Dante, letting him know this is his last chance to stop this.

He smirks and sits down on the couch next to Gia, pulling her into his lap. Using her as a shield in case this goes badly.

Coward.

He won't partake in what is about to happen, and he'd prefer his whore get shot, rather than him, if a bullet goes awry.

He doesn't think I'm the best if he thinks that's even a possibility of that happening.

"Dante, I'll get to work then," I say, giving my team the signal.

All at once we reach for our hidden weapons and begin taking out our targets one by one with silenced pistols. Most of Dante's men shout out and surround him. That's why my best people are with me. I take out three as I head toward the kitchen, knowing there are two more in there.

A bullet whizzes by my head as I duck and shoot the bastard dead with one quick shot to the head.

Another gets a bullet to the heart.

I hear my team all confirming their targets are down, but it doesn't make me drop my gun. Not until I get the all clear from Steward, my man monitoring the security system to ensure every man is down.

"You have one more in the hallway," Steward says.

My heart races, and my lips curl into a wicked smile. I enjoy this more than I should.

I move to the wall as I slink down the kitchen counters to the hallway where my last target awaits his death.

I turn the corner and fire before he has a chance to move or shoot. I watch his body drop to the floor in front of me.

"All clear," Steward says.

"And our team?" I ask, hoping my team has kept our flawless record of being injury free.

"All good. No injuries reported."

I let out a deep exhale. I take pride in not losing anyone on my team.

I walk back to the living room where Adela and Terence are waiting for me.

"It's done?" Dante asks.

I nod. "All of your men have been taken care of. I'll have my team dispose of the bodies and get your new team ready to go within the hour."

Dante grins as he fondles Gia's breasts much too hard. She doesn't move or flinch, if she notices his touch.

"What do you think, sweetheart?" Dante asks Gia, calling her an endearment for the first time; his tone conflicting with the dead men covering the floor.

"I think you are a coward."

I smirk. I can't help it. I agree with her assessment.

Dante doesn't notice. He's too intrigued by his plaything to notice me.

God, I have to have Gia.

It will fuck up all of my plans if I steal her from Dante. Plans I have been working on for years. I no longer care.

I stare at my sister out of the corner of my eye. I will need her help. I can't do this without her. She will hate me for doing this, but I can't help myself. And in the end, my sister will do anything for me.

But will I make her?

Yes.

I stare at the stunning brunette, who deserves so much better, but she will never get it.

I will steal Gia. I just have to be careful, so Dante doesn't realize I'm the one who stole her. And then, when I need to get in Dante's favor, I will return her. Pretend some other bastard was the culprit of her disappearance.

But how can someone steal her and my security team not be blamed?

"I'm taking my whore to my work while you finish. Call me when it's done."

I smirk. I have to steal her. *Now.* I'm not responsible for his security at his office. I have no cameras or security set up there. He can't blame me.

Dante forces Gia up. I don't know how she's standing. I'm pretty sure her legs are broken. She's fucking amazing, that's how.

And she's *mine*.

Gia will think I'm saving her when I steal her from Dante. But really, she'll be trading in one monster for another. One with the power to actually break her.

6

———

GIA

WORTHLESS. That's what Dante thinks I am. That's what my brain tells me my body is. My legs, my arms, my eyes; all broken, futile, and useless.

It's not the first time I've heard the word used. Enrico used to call me worthless all the time. I was no use to him. I was a daughter, not a son. I wasn't built for this world.

Enrico said I'm too stupid to understand the business.

Not strong enough to handle the bloodshed.

Not powerful enough to control a team of men.

Not smart enough to make high paying deals.

And I'm too pretty to be taken seriously.

My entire life I've been 'worthless.'

My brothers never said it, but they kept me out of the business as much as possible.

Now, Dante is saying the same things. I'm worthless. Nothing but a whore.

My mind believes him. I'm too broken to remember any of the reasons I am worthy. All I can think about is my faults. My body doesn't work. I'm so bruised and beat up no one would consider me beautiful anymore. I don't have a college degree. I

55

don't have a career. I don't even own a house or car anymore. I live off my inheritance. Inheritance I gained from a father who never loved me and brothers willing to do anything to keep me safe.

I should be defeated, but every time I hear the word 'worthless,' it sparks something in my heart. Something that keeps me alive. Makes me fight.

I think Dante knows what the word does to me, which is why he keeps using it.

Dante had his entire team killed in front of me. It was a warning. The same fate awaits me if I don't do as I'm told. But it didn't scare me.

It just made the fire in my heart grow with the need of my revenge. I don't know what the men did to deserve death, but I know if they willingly worked for Dante, they deserved their fate.

It didn't make me sad. It made me happy to see their karma repaid.

And now, I have a chance at freedom and my vengeance.

Dante is in the driver's seat of his white Maserati while I sit in the passenger seat with my head against the window, soaking up every drop of sunlight hitting the window. I won't move my head no matter how uncomfortable the crick in my neck grows, or how much my forehead burns from the light. Dante thinks I'm resting my head against the window because I'm too weak to move my head, but I'm drawing as much strength as I can from the sun's warmth, preparing for the coming battle.

This is the first time I've been out of the house since Dante stole me. He doesn't have any guards with us. They are all dead.

He didn't use any ropes to tie my arms or legs.

He carried me to the car because I can't walk.

We are headed to his office so he can enjoy me, while Conti and his team prepare a new security system and team of guards.

We will be alone. I may not be able to walk, but I'll fly when the opportunity arises for me to escape.

I sigh. Large trees block some of my sunlight as we drive through a wooded portion of the road, but it doesn't stomp my hope. The trees are picturesque Italian. The vines climbing up their trunks remind me of my homeland. I was never meant to be an American like my brothers have accepted. I'm meant to be an Italian. Whatever faces me, at least it will be here, in the motherland.

My eyes begin to drift shut, but I force them to stay wide. I don't want to miss a second of the beautiful countryside or the quaint cottages we'll pass on the side of the road. I try to memorize the path we are taking. All the houses and villages we pass become ingrained in my mind. If I get a chance to escape, I need to be able to find my way to help.

Dante pulls the car to a stop in front of a row of office buildings, and my heart sinks. Surely, there are going to be people everywhere. I won't have a chance to escape. I could make a run for it now, but I have no shot against Dante, not in my state.

He would punish me worse if I ran. And I don't think I can handle any more broken bones.

Dante gets out, without a word, and then walks to my side of the car, opening the door and lifting me gently into his arms.

I let my body remain limp. I will not use an ounce of energy that isn't necessary. But I don't know why he is acting so cautiously with me. Are we being watched?

I look around for a sign of a video camera I can make a plea for help to, but I find none.

No, Dante wouldn't work at a place where there are video cameras he doesn't own.

He pulls a key out of his pocket and unlocks the glass doors.

Why does he need to unlock a door, if this is an office building full of people?

"Don't worry, whore. It's Saturday. The building is closed on Saturdays. We are all alone. No one will hear your screams."

I bite my lip as if he's going to make me scream right now. He's not. He's gentle so that when he beats me, it will make it feel so much worse.

My arms and legs dangle as he pushes the door open, and we step inside the building. The smell of paper and air fresheners overwhelms my nose. It's such a stark difference to the smell of blood and musky men.

This place is clean and sterile. Dante doesn't bother to flick on the lights as he carries me down the hallway. He doesn't look at me or speak as he stomps. He's a man on a mission. I don't have to look into his eyes to know the carnage that happened only minutes ago turned him on. Dante loves the blood, the pain, the wrath. It's who he is. He enjoys killing.

He wants to take that all out on me. All of his lust and aggression.

Just as Dante said, we don't pass anyone as we head down two hallways, then into an elevator, and up five floors. I don't know what Dante does to make his money. This building doesn't add any clues. But if I had to guess, Dante's business is similar to my own family's business. Dante just isn't as good at selling weapons as we are. This building is a front; something he can point to when his more nefarious dealings are revealed to the police.

It's stupid. The police will never believe him. He needs to have the cops on his side as the Carinis have for years.

Dante opens a glass door to a large office. Glass walls surround us, while large windows open the office up to the outside light.

My eyes widen, and my mouth hangs open, as I stare at the office. It's so normal, bright, and airy. This cannot be Dante's office. He likes dark. He likes to hide in a cave. He would never work somewhere so open.

I glance up as Dante's eyes are searing into my body. I'm wearing clothes for the first time in weeks. It's just a T-shirt and his boxers, but I'm still thankful to be wearing clothes instead of being naked. But I know from the look in his eyes I won't be wearing them for much longer.

My body stills as he tosses me onto a leather couch. He removes his jacket, slowly, as he walks over to his desk. He's going to rape me again. I can't take it. Not even one more time.

My eyes scan his entire office in seconds, looking for a weapon. Scissors, a knife, a hidden gun. Even a stapler. I'll take anything I can use to inflict pain on this man.

Dante begins rolling up the sleeves of his crisp white shirt while he stands behind his desk. He bites his lip, and his entire face tightens as looks at me. But he's not really looking at me. He's envisioning his sick fantasy in his head. I've seen the disgusting look before.

I pull my legs up against my chest, wrapping my arms around them. It takes a lot of effort to move this little, but it's worth it to bring myself some level of comfort.

"Oh, so many things I could do to you, whore," Dante says.

My bottom lip trembles as his eyes go wild. I bite my lip, stilling it.

I will not be afraid.

Dante opens a drawer at the bottom of his desk. I try not to focus on what he's pulling out. It's meant to frighten me, as is everything he does around me. I will not let him win.

I try staring out the beautiful glass windows, filled with the warmth of the sunlight from the cloudless day. But I still see the items out of the corner of my eye, as he lays them on his desk.

A whip. Metal handcuffs. A butt plug. A ball gag. And a knife.

The knife is the only item that makes me react. He used it before on my back. It terrifies me. But it also excites me, for some reason.

My breathing speeds to unthinkable levels. My eyes water with both fear and excitement at seeing a weapon I could use against him. And my hands tremble in my lap.

The day he used the knife was the worst day. Unlike the pain of broken bones or rape that I can easily hide away within the cloud of overwhelming pain. The sharp edge of the blade can't be hidden. When it pierces my skin, there is no escape.

I cried. I screamed. I begged.

It was Dante's best day. My lowest point.

I can't relive it.

But it's a weapon. If I was able to get hold of the knife, I could kill Dante. I could get free.

I purse my lips and let all of the air out of my lungs, sinking into the couch and allowing all my muscles to relax. I haven't sat on anything this comfortable in weeks. I'm going to savor it.

I hear Dante's footsteps getting closer from behind the desk. I should pay attention to his movements so I can react and try to prevent an injury. My reflexes aren't what they used to be, though. So even if I know a punch or kick is coming, I can't move out of the way fast enough. I've learned to not spend any energy on avoiding his movements.

"We have hours together, undisturbed. We have an empty building. And new toys to play with."

I see Dante spin the knife in his hand. It's bigger than the last one he used.

Good. It will be easier to kill him with it.

A haunting song jolts us both out of our fantasies as his pocket rings and vibrates. He reaches into his back pocket and pulls the phone out. I think he's going to end the call without answering.

Instead, he answers.

"Perfect timing. I need an update before I turn off my phone for a few hours," Dante says, his lips curling up into a wicked grin to match the darkness in his eyes.

I grab the throw pillow on the couch and place it in front of my stomach, squeezing hard, like the pillow will somehow protect me from the dangers ahead.

Dante smirks, lifts the phone from his ear, and says, "That pillow won't save you, whore. I need to step outside to take this call. When I return, I expect you will be naked, and your cunt dripping wet, waiting for my cock."

I grimace as a low growl escapes my stomach.

Dante's stare intensifies. "If not, I will punish you." His eyes shine with a new level of hatred as he speaks. It would ruin his fucking plans if I were naked and my cunt was dripping for him.

He steps out the glass doors, and I almost consider stripping and doing everything possible to make my pussy wet for him. It would be worth it to see the surprise on his face, but he'd probably punish me anyway.

I watch as Dante paces outside the glass door. *Stupid, fucking glass.* What was so beautiful a minute ago has quickly lost its appeal. If it was sheetrock, then I could slink across the wooden floor to his desk and retrieve the knife without him noticing.

Maybe I still can?

If I had the knife, I could kill him. Or at the least injure him.

But if he caught me, it would be so much worse.

I try to still my body and become invisible. Dante isn't paying me any attention. Whoever is on the phone has Dante captivated.

Dante frowns and then keeps walking, out of view.

My heart stops. He left me alone.

He didn't tie me up.

I'm alone with a weapon.

I don't know how long he's going to be gone, but I won't wait to see.

This is my chance.

I force my body up from the couch. I expect unthinkable pain to roll through my body and drop me back to the couch, but I feel nothing.

Adrenaline or hope has filled my body, making it impossible for me to feel pain.

I grin, my cheeks flush, and my body moves. *This ends today.* I'm either going to be free or die trying.

I race across the room to snatch the knife. I move too fast and too slow at the same time. In reality, I have no idea how fast I walk.

I keep one eye on the glass wall, expecting Dante to return into view at any second. When my hand grasps the smooth surface of the black handle of the knife, I feel hope. Real *hope.*

I can escape.

I grip the knife firmly in my hand as I face the door. I could wait for Dante to return and stab him the second he enters. Or I could take my chance and run.

I tiptoe to the door, keeping the knife hidden down by my side as I lean against the door to see if Dante is just outside the door.

The hallway is empty.

My hands are sweaty as I work to hold onto the knife. I don't have much strength. I'm standing purely on adrenaline.

If Dante returns, it will take everything I have to stab him. It will just be luck whether I kill him or not.

I'm not waiting.

I glance back at his desk and notice a pair of keys. When did he toss his car keys onto his desk?

I don't bother trying to remember. I grab the keys with my other hand, and then, after taking one breath filling my body with every drop of air in the room to give me the courage to step into the hallway, I push the door open.

I open it slowly, ensuring any creaks of the door remain silent.

Silence.

I step out, holding onto the door as it carefully closes.

Silence.

I look to the left and then right. Dante disappeared to the right. So my feet move left.

Slow at first. Careful, cautious. But after two steps, I can't wait to get to freedom. I run or fly. I don't know which. All I know is my body soars down the hallway and to the elevator. The doors open the second I press the button, and I step inside. My pulse fires through my body as my mind flutters with thoughts of everything that could go wrong.

I press the ground floor button and catch my breath while the elevator descends. I don't know what is waiting for me when the doors open downstairs, but I hold the knife out, ready to attack.

The doors finally open, after what seems like years to my anxious body.

Nothing.

I don't have time to revel in another win. My feet run again. Legs, which aren't broken, compel my body forward, step after step. And even if my legs are broken, they work anyway.

I zero in on the door, only glancing to my left when I pass the final hallway before reaching the door.

Nothing. No one.

I don't hesitate as I push the door open and step out into the sunlight. I want to lie flat on the concrete and let the sun heal me, but I'll have to wait until I'm somewhere safer.

My feet keep moving quickly as I grab the door handle of the

Maserati Dante drove me here in. I pull on the handle, but it doesn't open.

I frown.

Dante has one of these keyless entries. The kind that you don't have to press a button to enter the car. You only need to have the keys on you, and the doors unlock automatically.

I fidget with the keys, find the fob, and press the unlock button. Then, I grab the door handle again and pull.

It doesn't budge.

Shit.

I press the button over and over, but nothing happens. I try inserting the key into the door, but it doesn't fit.

These keys don't belong to the Maserati.

I look around the parking lot, but there is only one other car. A Fiat. I press the unlock button again, but the car is silent as well. It doesn't come to life.

Dante didn't pull these keys out of his pocket. These keys belong to a different car or a different owner.

I throw the keys at Dante's Maserati, watching as a tiny dent forms.

I smile a minuscule amount. The first smile I can recall in a month. A dent in his precious car is sure to enrage him.

My feet start flying again, as I move out of the parking lot to the road. I don't see or hear cars coming in either direction. I have two choices. Run along the road and hope I run into someone who can help me, or disappear into the woods.

I chose a man last time to help me. It was a mistake. This time, I choose me. I choose the woods. I'll disappear into the woods. Hopefully, Dante will think I chose the road. I'll hide in the woods for a couple of days until I can find a way to get to a phone.

I run across the road and disappear into the woods. I glance behind me but don't see anyone following me.

I'm free.

I take another step though, and my legs give out. It's almost as if they only had the strength to make it to the edge of freedom, but not enough to finish the job.

NO! *Get up.*

I grab onto a tree trunk and force myself to stand again. I can't keep running. I have to take things slowly. Very, very slowly. I hate it, but I don't have a choice.

It's okay. I have time. Dante will look here last. I need to find a place to hide in. I could gather some leaves and cover myself and hide until dark falls. Give my legs some rest; then I might be able to move again.

Or I could freeze or starve to death.

I need to keep moving for as long as I can.

"Stop."

My legs stop at the command. It's what they are desperate for: a reason to stop. They've done so much and gotten me so far, but they aren't enough to take me miles from here.

I grip the knife tighter in my hand as it rests by my side. I don't know if the man behind me has seen the blade or not. I don't know if the man behind me is my foe or friend. I lean toward foe.

I settle my breathing, trying to appear natural, but there is no way any person would take a look at me and think something isn't wrong.

I hear the crunch of leaves behind me as the man approaches me.

My jaw ticks, while the rest of my body remains still. I purse my lips again, letting all the anxiety out of me. One stab. I can get one stab in. It will give me an adrenaline rush again, and then I'll be able to run. I just have to wait until the man is close enough to stab.

More crunching of leaves, and then a hand on my shoulder.

I turn as fast as my body will allow me and bring the knife up to jab into the man's shoulder. I don't care if he is a friend. I don't trust anyone.

My knife dives toward him, but his hand grasps my wrist, inches before it plunges into his chest.

My eyes flicker to his.

Conti.

Fuck.

His eyes are unreadable as he stares at me, still holding onto my wrist.

I'm going back to Dante.

"Please," I whisper.

Conti's eyes narrow, but I don't have a clue what that means.

"Drop the knife."

I stare up at the knife. At my *salvation.*

"I can't."

He nods as if he understands.

"I'll let you run if you want to run, but Dante will find you before morning. He knows you are missing. That's why I'm here."

I nod.

"Or you can come with me."

I laugh. I don't know why. Maybe because I need the release. "I will never become Dante's again."

He nods. "I wasn't asking you to go back to Dante. I was asking you to be *mine.*"

"I don't want to belong to anyone. I want to be free."

"No one is ever free."

Sadness. That is what I see, mixed with lust, in his eyes.

"I was."

"No, you weren't. You belonged to the rich, the powerful. You belonged to your family. You never belonged to yourself."

"Why would I go with you? Why would I trust you? Last time you turned me over to Dante."

"Last time I didn't have a choice. I didn't know what I was giving up. Now I do. I want you, Gia Carini."

He knows my name, and it feels good to hear something other than cunt or whore. But he turned me over. He's raped me before.

"You're no better than him," I say, unable to speak the devil's name, or even think it for another second.

"No, I'm not better than him. In fact, I'm probably worse. I'm not saying I'm offering you deliverance. I'm not saving you. Just offering you a new master."

He speaks the truth. Every one of his words. I believe him.

"What will happen if I go with you, Conti? Will you rape me, torture me, and beat me?"

His jaw twitches.

"Maybe. Maybe, I'll do worse. And the name is Caspian. Conti is my father's name."

My face softens when I hear Caspian. I try to reread this man. Last time, I saw kindness. I saw hope. This time, I'm realistic. It wasn't kindness I saw before. It was pain and sadness. I see it now. Now that I've felt it.

This man is broken, same as me. He's not evil like Dante is. Caspian may not treat me well, but he won't hurt me in the same way Dante did.

Caspian may rape me, hurt me, beat me, but not with the same hatred. Caspian's rage comes from a place of pain. Pain can weaken, hate can't.

"Choose Gia. The woods, where Dante will find you, or me."

Nothing can be worse than Dante. I don't trust Caspian, but I believe him. I don't know what faces me, but I don't have a choice.

"You."

7

CASPIAN

I SHOULD BE OVERSEEING the security team. I should be at Dante's house ensuring the system I set up is working flawlessly. I should be on the phone with Dante, schmoozing him, and making sure he thinks everything I'm doing is to make him more secure.

Instead, I'm standing at the edge of the woods, while the most entrancing woman I've ever met tells me she will come with me.

I shouldn't be here.

I shouldn't steal Gia.

It could ruin *everything*.

Gia isn't the type of woman who is barely noticed. She blazes in, knocking down walls, and setting fire to everything in her path. Some people survive and are made stronger because she was in their life, but most dissolve into ashes.

Gia takes one step and her leg trembles. I've studied her body for the last three minutes, and I know her leg is broken. She can walk on it, but only because there is so much adrenaline pulsing through her veins. Adrenaline is the only thing keeping her moving. And it is almost gone. She won't be standing much longer.

I rush to her side, my arms finally able to wrap around her body again. I grab onto her waist, and her hands grip my forearms.

Gia is filthy. Covered in layers of dirt and mud. Her face is swollen, and about ten different shades of black and blue. The only thing left of the Gia I saw that day outside the coffee shop is her eyes. Her eyes still blaze with life.

Her hair, once straight and shiny, is now tangled and matted. I don't know if she will ever be able to get the knots out, except by cutting her hair. I can't even let my eyes travel over the rest of her body. My anger rages too fast in my chest at the number of cuts, bruises, and broken bones.

I can't think about what Dante did to her. It will destroy me.

I don't let Gia see my rage, instead, I still in strong solitude.

"I can walk," Gia says, her voice so fucking determined.

I chuckle. This is not the time for chuckling. If Dante changes his plans and decides to search these woods, he'll find us. And I won't have a choice, but to turn her back over to him.

"No, you can't."

I don't give her a choice. I scoop her up in my arms and start jogging back to my car, hidden under a large oak tree on the edge of the street.

Gia stops fighting once she's in my arms. She doesn't have a choice. I try to do anything to keep from looking at her. In just a few minutes, she'll be mine. Dante will have no chance to get her back. I can look at her all I want then. Do more than look at her.

Having Gia in my arms makes it impossible for me to focus though. All I can do is breathe in her scent. Before she smelt like roses. It still lingers in her hair, but now she reeks of Dante. Musky, sweaty, and manly.

I need to change that.

I bite my bottom lip to keep from growling as my legs move faster to get her away from this devil.

Gia doesn't move in my arms. She lays her head on my chest, and I know her eyes are open because I can feel them burning into a spot on my chin. Don't look at her.

I make it to my Fiat, and though I know she would be more comfortable in a backseat where she could lie down on the journey ahead, I'm glad my car doesn't have a backseat. I need her near me. I need to be able to touch her and keep my eyes on her as we drive. Otherwise, I'll lose my damn mind.

So that's where I put her, before hopping in the driver's seat. My heart pounds half from stress and half from anger. It's been a long time since I cared so much about a mission working out like this one. It takes everything inside of me not to call Dante and drive straight to him before pulling out my gun and shooting him dead.

How could he ever think it was okay to maim such a beautiful spirit?

"You going to drive or do I need to?" Gia says. She's slouched in the chair, not even able to hold her head up. There is no way she can drive. Her sly smile and rosy cheeks warm my heart.

He didn't damage her spirit. It's very much alive.

I speed out of our spot, slinging Gia against the window as I do.

"Much better," she says, as she slowly pushes herself off the window into an upright position.

I should drive her straight to the hospital. Her body is beaten so much; she no doubt needs countless surgeries to fix her broken bones.

It won't be safe.

The hospital would be one of the first places Dante looks.

That's what I keep telling myself anyway. The truth is I'm a selfish bastard who wants Gia all to myself.

"Where are we going?" Gia asks, her voice weaker than before. Everything she does drains another quarter of her energy. She should conserve it. Another sentence or two and she'll pass out from exhaustion.

"Shh, you should rest. You don't need to worry about anything. You're mine, now."

I expect her to listen. I know she feels safer than she did with Dante. And for the time being at least, she's right.

She doesn't listen.

"I'm not anyone's. I belong to me."

Focus on the road. There is no reason to argue semantics with her right now. She's mine, even if she won't say it.

But I see her damn lips curl up. She knows her not saying she's mine fucks with me.

I try to figure out what gave me away. Usually, only my sister can read me. My grip is loose on the steering wheel. I'm driving fast, but not excessive. My body is relaxed, sunk into my seat. And my facial expressions are blank.

Gia looks at me dreamily.

"What?" I snap a little too loudly.

This earns me a full smile. *Damn it.* She likes getting under my skin.

"Gia, I don't like being disobeyed. You will learn that soon. So when I ask you a question or give you a command, I expect you to follow it. Understand?"

She giggles. "Yes, sir."

I glare at her, unable to hold in my rage at her little mistake.

"Why are you giggling? You think me risking my life to take you is funny?"

She takes a deep breath, calming her giggles. "No."

I hesitate before asking my next question, but it's the one I want answered the most. "Are you afraid of me?"

She pauses. "No."

"Why not?"

"Because you call me Gia."

I shake my head. "That won't stop me from raping you when I get the chance. It won't stop my temper from beating you when you disobey me. It won't stop me from breaking you."

She nods. "Maybe not. But you call me Gia instead of whore. You see me as a human instead of property. That's a start. You can't be worse than him."

I shake my head. *She has no idea.*

My phone buzzes, right on cue. My car has the ability to answer calls hands-free, but I don't want Gia to hear; nor do I want Dante to have a chance at hearing Gia next to me.

So I retrieve my phone from my pocket and answer the call privately on my phone.

"Hello, Dante. What can I do for you?" I answer, loving how much it pisses him off to use Dante instead of Mr. Russo. It will never get old.

"You can get your fucking team to my office ASAP. My whore is missing. Stolen, no doubt. Your fucking fancy security system and team did nothing to stop it!"

I grin. I can't help myself at hearing his panic on the other end of the line. Even if I didn't want Gia for myself, I should have stolen her to listen to his panic.

"My team wasn't responsible for you or your whore's security this afternoon. I told you, you shouldn't have left the house until the team was set up to escort you."

"You don't get to fucking lecture me, Caspian. Not today! Fucking fix it, or your whole team is fired."

"I will have my team meet you at your office. We will find her. If she's still in Italy, we will find her."

"And if she's not?" Dante's voice trembles as he speaks.

"Then, we will find you a new whore while we track down her kidnapper and kill him."

I end the call. Pocketing my phone.

Her eyes are huge as she stares at me. Her smile has vanished. And she's now as far as she can get from me in her chair.

She's afraid of me. I don't have to ask her to understand that.

"You're going to return me to him..." Her lip quivers and tears threaten in her big green eyes, clouding the sparkle there before.

"No."

"I don't believe you. You turned me over to him before. You want to wait a few days. Get your fill of me, and then pretend you found me when it's most convenient to get back on Dante's good side."

"N—"

"I'll tell Dante. I'll tell him everything if you give me back to him."

I pull the car over abruptly to the side of the road. I need to focus on her if I'm going to win this fight with her.

I grab her shoulders and pull her, so she is staring straight at me. I tell myself it's so I have her full attention, and she can see into my eyes that I'm telling the truth, but it's because I need to have my hands on her.

"If you believe one thing about me, believe this. I will never give you back to Dante. Even to save my own skin. You will never see Dante Russo again. He will never touch you again. Never beat you. Never rape you. Once I claim something as mine, it's mine. I don't share. I don't change my mind. I will never let Dante have you again."

"Dante won't stop looking for me. Ever. You can't assure that."

I cock my head to the side and give her a wicked smirk I'm sure reaches my eyes. "I'm Dante's security now. He wiped out his old team. He trusts me. Dante will never find you unless I want him to find you. I control Dante now. And I'm the best damn security in the country. You are free of Dante."

My eyes scan hers, trying to decide if she believes me. I don't know why it matters to me that she believes me. It's frustrating me that I can't read her.

"Do you believe me?"

Nothing. No answer on her face or from her lips.

"Gia?" I ask, with a warning to my voice.

"I don't know."

I sigh.

"Why? Why would you never turn me over to Dante? I don't understand."

So many heartbreaking images fill my head, and I almost forget where I am.

I shake my head, pushing the memories away.

"It doesn't matter why. Just believe me when I say Dante will never own you again."

I release her, and her body falls back into the chair, unable to hold herself up. I start driving again while we both sit in silence.

I do everything I can to not think about the gorgeous, feisty woman sitting next to me. When my mind starts counting her breaths, I change to counting the road signs we pass. When my eyes cut to the glow of her filthy skin, I punish them by playing images of Dante. When my nose takes deeper breaths, trying to get a whiff of her sweet smell, I roll down my window as we pass a cow pasture.

It takes us forty-five minutes to reach the small turnoff for my house. Gia fell asleep shortly after driving again. Her breathing has been slow and steady since.

I reached over around minute ten to tuck her hair behind her ear so I could see her pretty face better. She didn't stir. I punished myself by digging my nails into my skin. I'm going to need a better way to keep Gia out of my thoughts when I'm on the job. This won't work.

Now that we are almost to my house, it doesn't matter if I think about her. I can act on my needs. Fuck her if I want.

No. I will not fuck a woman who was so recently touched by another man. He probably fucked her in his office before she ran.

I slow my speed as the car sways over the gravel path leading to my house. There is no sign for this road. There is barely even an opening among the trees. It's how I like it. No one knows my house even exists back here.

Slowly, my black roof starts peaking out over the trees. The small cabin-like feel of the siding comes into view.

"Your house is tiny."

My head jerks to Gia. I thought she was asleep, but the bouncing of the car must have woken her.

I raise an eyebrow. "I can return you to your previous owner. Just say the word, and you'll be back in his giant mansion."

She stills. "I'll give your tiny house a try first."

I narrow my eyes. "I forgot. You're a Carini. You care about things like houses and cars and money."

She looks out the window, suddenly more solemn. I said something wrong.

"I'm not sure if such things matter or not, but I miss them." The way she speaks with regret stirs my deep feelings. It's clear she doesn't want to miss mansions, money, and expensive cars.

I shrug. "I don't think it matters if you prefer giant mansions or not. I prefer my excluded house in the woods."

"Our house was excluded. Hidden. But it had enough rooms we could all live under one roof. My entire family. We could have extravagant parties and lush rooms. Why wouldn't you want that?"

I shake my head. "You may think the Carini mansion was hidden and private. It wasn't. Trust me. I've been doing security for a long time. I've seen hundreds of houses. My house is private. Yours wasn't."

"I doubt you have been doing this for a long time." She rakes her eyes over my body as she takes in my appearance and age.

"Security is all I've ever done. Even when I was a kid. Don't start judging me because I don't come from a long line of Conti's who work in security. I made my money on my own."

Her face brightens at my admission. *Damn it. How do I keep revealing so much about myself to her so easily?*

She nods. "I wasn't judging you for not inheriting money. I admire that. It seems like a simpler life, where nothing is expected of you, and you can choose your own path. I envy you for that."

"Don't. My life is no more perfect than yours is."

She raises an eyebrow. "You can't be serious. Your life is a lot better than mine. You've never had your life threatened. Your ownership of your body, taken. Never been violated by another person."

"Don't speak unless you know the words you are saying are truthful. You know nothing about my life. In some ways, my hell is much worse than yours."

Her eyes cross in confusion and her luscious red lips open to speak again. I climb out of the car before she starts firing off her questions. This is one area she won't be getting any answers to her questions. I've endured more pain than she can ever imagine. I would easily trade paths with her to get rid of my own omnipresent pain.

I walk to her side, but her door is already open, and her feet are swung to the side as she prepares to step out.

Not fucking happening.

I scoop her up roughly.

"Put me down. I can walk! There is no threat at the moment. Dante isn't lurking behind one of the trees. Let me walk. It doesn't matter how long it takes me."

"It does too matter how long. I have work to do. I can't just sit around waiting for hours as you stumble into my house."

She pouts. "What did you mean back there about your hell being worse?"

I refuse to answer her or even acknowledge her words. I enter my code on the front door and wait for the door to unlock after it has scanned my face and recognized me as the owner. It opens, and I carry her in. The door shuts and locks automatically behind me.

"Caspian, it's good to have you home. Can I get you anything, sir?" Michi, my assistant, and the owner of the house on paper, asks. He oversees everything that has to do with the house when I'm not here.

"We would love some food. Something light, please Michi."

Gia looks from me to Michi curiously. I expect her to open her mouth, but she doesn't.

"Yes, sir. I'll make some soup and grilled cheese."

"Thank you."

Michi heads to the kitchen.

"Wow, I'm surprised you can fit a third person into this shack," Gia says, with a hint of teasing in her voice. I don't know what it is that allows her to feel comfortable teasing me, but I like it.

"Watch it, or you'll be sleeping outside."

I carry her to my bedroom. The house is small, with only two bedrooms; one for me and one for Michi. The living room couch folds out into a bed when my sister stays over. But that isn't often anymore. I didn't think about it much when I was planning on taking Gia, just that I wanted her here.

I'll figure out the rest later. I place her on my bed before I realize my mistake. My cock comes to life straining hard in my pants at the sight of her on my bed.

The T-shirt she is wearing doesn't hide her glorious tits. Her nipples are hard against the thin material. And the boxers she is wearing cling to her far too skinny legs. Legs that were not this skinny before, but after a month of hardly eating, I'm sure she has lost a lot of weight.

I frown. I need the clothes off of her, but I don't want this to be a fight. She's exhausted, and my temper is tired of being tested. I'm not used to anyone disobeying my commands. She will learn to follow my demands, but it will take time.

Today, I want her clean, in new clothes, and fed. Then I will busy myself in work or spend my night jerking off while I try to be patient and not claim her pussy tonight.

I leave her on my bed, knowing full well she will try to get up and make a run for it. My bathroom is good sized. Not huge, but it has a large clawfoot tub I never use. Now I'm glad I never got rid of it to make more space in the bathroom.

I turn on the faucet in the tub and stick my hand under the water until it is warm, but not hot. I don't think her skin can handle hot. I take my time returning to the bedroom. I lean against the door frame watching her as it takes everything in her to scoot herself to the edge of the bed.

"What is your plan once you are standing?"

Her body jumps at the sound of my voice. She looks up with a frown.

I smile. "What's your plan? I know you don't have a weapon. You haven't figured out where I keep my guns yet. You can barely walk. If you run, I'd get you back in five minutes. What's your plan?"

"Dante didn't find me in five minutes when I ran."

I nod. "True, but then you weren't the one that planned your escape. I did."

Her frown deepens, and the determination in her eyes grows stronger. "You did not plan my escape, *I* did."

I smirk. "I had my team call, Dante, to distract him so you could escape. I made sure no one was in that building or parking lot. I made sure he didn't find you."

"I escaped on my own."

"Fine. You made it down an elevator, through a parking lot, and into the woods. If it weren't for me, you would have died in those woods or Dante would've found you."

She folds her arms across her chest, hiding her view of her breasts from me.

My lips thin, but I don't frown. I don't want her to see my disappointment at her hiding her body from me.

"What's your plan? You aren't escaping. You aren't strong enough. So I would recommend you let me help you clean up, you eat some food, and you rest. And then, when you've healed, you can try an escape again. Okay, sweetheart?"

Her jaw twitches when I say 'sweetheart.' She clearly doesn't like nicknames. But she doesn't say anything.

"I'm going to remove your clothes and help you into the tub so we can clean the filth off you."

I walk to her not giving her a choice in the matter as I grab the hem of her T-shirt. She keeps her arms crossed and I give her a stern look.

"Do you want to waste energy fighting me on this? You want to be clean. And I can't leave you alone in the bathtub. You'd drown. So let me help you."

Slowly, she lifts her arms and lets me remove her shirt. She doesn't shudder or hide when my eyes rake over her body. She's used to being naked in front of men.

My cock grows, but it stills every time a new bruise or injury is revealed. I don't think there is one area of her skin that hasn't been touched by that monster.

I kneel down in front of her as I grab the waistband of his boxers. She lifts her hips the tiniest bit as I pull them off her. My eyes go to her beautiful cunt. Needing to see it. It's glorious. But then my eyes see the large bruise on the inside of her thigh. I see the red cuts around her ankles and wrists where she's been tied up too tightly. I see the way her knee bends at an awkward angle, clearly not set correctly.

Fuck.

Her body is more damaged than I ever imagined possible. I don't know how her body hasn't already shut down from the pain.

I hoped to see the naked body of the beautiful woman who fell into my lap and begged for my help. Now that body is so scarred, there are only remnants left. She needs to heal.

My cock stiffens at the sight of her nipples hardening in the brisk air.

Damn, cock.

I can't fuck her. Not here. Not now. I'm better than this.

Our gazes meet, exchanging too many feelings. I hate feelings. I don't do feelings. Not anymore. I've spent the last few years shut off from the world. The only emotion I ever felt was anger and revenge.

Now, looking at Gia as I stand over her, she stirs a feeling I haven't felt in years. I can't quite place it. I don't know what the feeling is called. I hate it. I want it to go away. But I need to wash away any sign of Dante from her body. Or at least, what I can wash away. I know I can't remove the bruises or scars. Or the mental images from her mind.

I see the same emotion in Gia's eyes. Revenge is what she

runs on. It's what has kept her alive, but there is something different now.

"Thank you," she says quietly.

I still. She shouldn't thank me. Not until she understands what I require of her. Not until she knows who I am. But I recognize it as the feeling in her eyes. She's thankful. Her eyes say she's scared to say the words, but she says them because it releases her from any guilt over what comes next.

I feel the reflection of emotion in myself. I'm grateful I have her. That I could save her, whatever that means.

I will accept that I did save her. Dante was set on killing her. Doing everything he could to get to that point and push her over the edge to darkness until her body stopped working, her mind shut down, and she vanished into nothing. If I hadn't saved her, I'm not sure she would have survived another week. Definitely not another month.

"You're welcome," I say, finally admitting what I've done.

Gia moves to get off the bed but then stops herself. She looks up at me with her dopey sad eyes. Her eyes say sad, but her long curling eyelashes say beautiful. I could get lost in the length of her lashes.

She exhales deeply, but it comes out more of a huff of frustration.

"Caspian, will you please help me to the bath?"

I catch my breath in my throat. Of all the things I expected her to say, I never expected her to ask for my help. I don't know what I did to earn her trust, but at this moment, she's giving it to me.

I don't say a word. I put one hand under her frail legs and the other under her arms. I lift her, feeling every bone in her body pressing into my chest as I carry her.

I've fantasized about carrying her naked since I first saw her. But this is the opposite of what I wanted. This is me taking care of her. This will hurt her worse than any physical thing I could do for her. She can't feel anything when it comes to me. She can't like me, or be grateful for me, or love me.

I place her into the warm water of the bath, carefully lowering her as her hands grasp onto the side of the tub to keep herself upright. I turn the faucet off as the water covers her breasts.

I kneel next to the tub. I can't leave her alone because she could drown, I tell myself. No matter how weak Gia's body is now, she would never let herself drown. She's too strong for that. Her spirit won't allow it.

Gia closes her eyes and lays her head against the back of the tub, letting the warm water go to work on her body and soul. The water immediately turns a light brown color as the caked on dirt washes off her skin.

I hold out a bar of soap and wait until she opens her eyes to take it from my hand. She begins moving the bar over her arms and chest, shakily rubbing her skin with the soap. She winces with every tiny movement, either from the energy it takes to move her arm or the pain the bar of soap causes as it moves over her skin.

I can't keep watching.

My hand reaches out to grab the soap from her, gripping her hand over the soap resting against her chest.

Her eyes meet mine, and I think she's going to fight me. Tell me she can wash herself. But she slowly relinquishes the bar of soap to me.

My teeth clench together, and my cock is hard as a rock as I move the soap over her chest to wash off the dirt. She watches me a moment. Staring into my eyes like she will find the greatest treasure if she keeps looking. Luckily, my waist is hidden from her view by the side of the tub. She can't see how hard I am for her and how desperate I am to become Dante. To rip her from the tub and fuck her. If Dante hadn't already hurt her so much, I would probably be doing just that.

Slowly, Gia closes her eyes and rests her head back while I move as slowly as I can to wash her. Applying just enough pressure to clean away the dirt, while careful not to press too hard and cause her more pain.

Every once in a while she bites her lip, winces, or lets out a low moan when I press too hard. But for the most part, I feel like I'm in more pain than she is.

"I need you to sit up so I can wash your back."

She opens her eyes slowly, as if even doing something that simple hurts. I've never been in that much physical pain before, so it's hard for me to understand. I do understand emotional distress, however.

She grabs onto the side of the tub again and starts pulling while I put my hand on the smoothness of her back and push her into a sitting position. Her entire body trembles as I wash her back. I move quickly so she can relax again.

I put the soap away and grab the nearby bottle of shampoo. It's not a feminine scent. It's the kind I use. Fresh and manly. She will smell like me if I use it, and I can't resist.

She notices the shampoo and dunks her head under the water to soak her long tresses. I squeeze a couple of drops of the shampoo into my hand and then massage it into her hair, hoping it will work on the tangles as well as the dirt.

Gia moans loudly.

"Am I hurting you?" I ask, stopping, afraid she has an injury covered by her hair.

She smiles up at me sweetly. "No, sorry. You massaging my head like that feels incredible."

My jaw falls open a little when I massage the shampoo into her head again, and the same sound escapes her lips. It sounds like I'm doing much more to her body than just shampooing her hair. It sounds like I'm rubbing an area much further south. I can only imagine the sounds she makes when she comes.

I sigh. I need to wait days, weeks, months until I try to hear those types of sounds from her. And even then, I don't think she will find sex with me enjoyable enough to gasp and moan at my touch. She will probably fight me off, instead.

I finish shampooing and help her dunk her hair back, rinsing the suds from her hair.

She runs her hands through her hair, working to untangle the strands.

"Give it time," I say when I see the disappointment at her hair not untangling.

She nods.

We both need to give ourselves time.

I grab a towel from the cabinet while we wait for the water to drain out of the tub. When the tub is empty of water, I wrap the towel around her and carry her back to my bed. I sit her on the edge of the bed and help her dry her body and hair before I head to my drawers and pull out one of my T-shirts and boxer shorts. It feels strange to be giving her the same thing to wear Dante gave her.

But when I hold out the clothes for her, she takes them with a warm smile.

I help her put the clothes on and climb into the bed.

Her eyes fall closed the second her head hits the pillow.

"I'll have Michi bring you food soon."

"Mmm."

I crack a tiny grin. I don't know why you are in my life, Gia Carini, but you have turned all my plans upside down. I'm not even sure what I want with you, beautiful. My cock knows what he wants. But what do I want? Why did I take you? Why did I save you? And what happens next?

I sit in my favorite chair in the living room with a scotch in my hand. It's late. Almost three in the morning, but I prefer the night. I like the darkness. It hides my emotions well. No one can discover any of my secrets if they are buried beneath the dark blanket of night.

I stare at my bedroom door I closed hours ago. Gia slept for two hours before I woke her to eat the soup and grilled cheese sandwich Michi cooked. She's been asleep since after she finished her dinner. I considered sleeping in the bed next to her, but I stopped myself. I didn't care if she was comfortable or not, but I knew if I slept in the same bed with her I wouldn't be able to control myself. Fucking her will be so much better when she's healed.

Instead, I sit in my chair drinking my scotch. It's not an expensive brand. I don't drink it for the taste. I drink it because it dulls my emotions. So why bother buying an expensive bottle?

I have a theory about Gia Carini. I think I know her better than she realizes. I've barely spent any time with her, but I know enough. My job is about reading people, and I can read her like an open book. The signs are all there. I don't have to read the file I had Adela do on her to know who Gia Carini is. She may have thanked me for helping her escape this evening, but that was then. I don't expect any more thank yous. From now on, the real Gia will come out. The one that will do whatever it takes to save herself.

I don't have a TV, and even if I did, I wouldn't turn it on to help the minutes pass. I don't open a book or play music either. All that I have to pass the time with is my scotch and the ticking of the clock in my living room. It's enough. Just thinking about Gia is enough.

I hear the familiar crick of the door.

I don't react. I don't smile or frown. I don't gasp or growl. This was what I was expecting.

The door cracks open further until I can see the shadow of Gia standing in the doorway holding onto the doorway like it's a lifeline.

Anger and annoyance roll through me. Gia may be brave, but she's also stubborn and relentless, both will eventually get her killed.

I nurse my drink while I watch Gia in the darkness gather her strength. She holds onto the wall as she takes careful steps, trying to quiet her feet on my old battered floors. It's an impossible task for the talent of a ballerina floating across the floor, let alone someone who is injured. Gia can't control her legs. She's off balance, and every step sounds like an elephant tromping through my house.

She falls. I hear the thunderous sound vibrate through the entire house, her body hitting the ground.

I wince and curse under my breath. My instinct is to run to her and help her up. I'm desperate to help her.

That's what I'm doing, I remind myself. By staying, I'm helping her.

So I wait and force more of the cheap scotch down my throat. She gets back to her feet, but it takes time. I've already finished my drink, poured myself a second, and finished all but a drop of that before she manages to stand again.

I close my eyes. I feel her heavy breathing. I hear her bones aching with each movement. My floor bends and cracks with each shift of her weight.

I grip the armrests, trying to restrain myself. *Stay. Wait.*

I glance up at the clock above my fireplace mantel. It's after four in the morning. She's been at this almost an hour now. *Enough.*

I spring off of my chair and walk silently into the hallway.

"Fifty-five minutes and thirty-four seconds, that must be a world record for the slowest attempt at escaping my house," I snarl. I can't keep my anger and frustration out of my voice, though I know it will provoke her temper.

Gia glares at me, her anger reaching the deepest parts of her frown.

"If you've been listening to me this entire time, you could have at least helped me back to bed or told me there was no point."

I laugh in a twisted way. "Would you have listened or would you have just postponed your attempt until tomorrow?"

She crosses her arms across her chest as her mouth prepares to tell me off, but the movement knocks her off balance.

I grab her before she falls again. I sigh. "Stop trying to escape. Stop trying to save yourself. It won't work. You're too weak."

She chuckles in defeat. "Would you stop fighting? How can I stop when it's all I have? I have my freedom, my honor, my name. That's all I am. I'm Gia Carini. Wealthy, powerful, and beautiful. If I lose it, then what?

"I have nothing left. I have to fight. I can't spend tonight giving into you when tomorrow you could be beating me half to death. If that happens, I need to know I did everything I could to try and escape tonight. Understand?"

"More than you know."

"So don't lecture me about trying to escape."

I shake my head. "You need to stop trying to escape. No matter what happens next, you are still Gia Carini, the most powerful, intelligent, beautiful woman in all of Italy. Nothing I do will change that. But you have to stop trying to escape. You'll never heal."

"Why would I want to heal when you will just break me again? I see it in your eyes. I know you are just as bad as Dante, even if you can control yourself better than him. Why wait for you to lose control?"

"Because like you said, I can control my monster. I won't hurt you. For one month."

Her eyes widen, and her mouth falls open. And all I can think about is what it would feel like to shove my cock into her glorious mouth. Her long pink tongue massaging me, bringing me to the brink.

"Caspian?"

She must have said something.

"Yes?"

She shakes her head. "I thanked you for saving me, or whatever it was when you took me from Dante. But that doesn't make you a saint."

"I never said it did."

"Then let me go. You have no use for me. You are a good-looking man. I'm sure you can get plenty of women. You have enough money you can pay a nice woman to live out your fantasies. You don't need me. Call my brothers. Tell them I'm safe and for them to rescue me. You don't need the hassle. If Dante finds out you have me, your business will be ruined, and you will probably end up dead."

I don't disagree with her. She's right. But again I think too much with my cock, and all I can think about is she called me good-looking. I think back to the day we first met. The look of lust in her eyes I thought I imagined. Was that real?

"No."

It's a simple word that answers her unspoken question.

She doesn't react to my word. She knew it would be my answer. It's why she never asked the question. It's why she tried to sneak out in the middle of the night.

"I can promise you this, Gia. I won't touch you. I won't hurt you. Nothing. For one month.

"For one month you can move about this house as if you aren't enslaved. For one month you can have as much freedom as you like within these four walls. Come and go in any room as you please. Ask Michi to make you any food you want. Ask me to do anything within reason for you in this house. Heal. Stop trying to sneak out.

"Then, after the month is up, you are free to try and run as much as you want. But when the month is up, attempting to run will be as useless as it is now. Your body can't handle running now, but even if you were healed, I have the best security system installed in my house. Better than ones I install in any of my clients' homes. You will never escape without my permission."

"Why?"

I shake my head. I just told her she was safe for an entire month, and she asks me why. She's too curious for her own good. She should accept my offer and work for the next month to figure out my weaknesses, instead of using all her strength to stand in this dark hallway and talk to me.

"Does it matter?"

"Yes," she says without hesitation.

"I don't play with broken toys, even partially broken."

She narrows her eyes into thin slits. Her eyes are the only thing I can see in the dark of the night, and now they are barely visible.

"I'm entirely broken."

"No!" My voice is louder than I wanted when I opened my mouth, and her body jumps. I slow and calm my voice. "You are not broken. Just injured. You can heal."

She shivers under my gaze. "When the month is up, will you hurt me?"

Yes. No. I don't know. I can't tell her any of those things. I don't even know what I want myself. But the answer is most likely yes.

"I have a track record of hurting women. I've never failed."

"Neither has Dante. Dante always ends the lives of the women he captures within a month. He failed."

She's hoping I'll admit I, too, will fail. But hurting her isn't my mission, unlike Dante. I will wound her whether I want to or not. Her being in my life will mean she will end up fatally injured, forever.

"Dante never played with your heart."

She gasps. I got the reaction I wanted, now time to close.

"He fought to get it, but he never had it. You can't take a heart by force. It has to be given, *willingly*. I don't just want your body Gia. I want all of you. Your heart most of all. And I'm the type of man who won't give up until I have it."

"And if you claimed my heart?"

"I would never give it back. I don't think you've ever lived without your heart. It's like living in the dark shadows, never being able to step into the light. It's not a particularly enjoyable way to live."

She silently nods like she understands. She doesn't. I've seen women lose their minds by the time I'm done with them. They leave me more broken than the woman leaving Dante's side. Death is the only answer for someone who has lost the will to live.

"Hold onto your heart, Gia. Don't give it to me. And don't let me steal it. If you want to live after you leave here, then keep yourself guarded. And when the month is up, find a way to escape."

8

———

GIA

A MONTH IS A LONG TIME, but at the same time, not long enough. Especially when I've spent most of my month in bed. I've never slept so much in all of my life.

When my body hits the bed, I'm out. It doesn't matter what plans I had before. Once I'm in Caspian's bed, I'm out.

When I leave, I'm stealing this bed. Caspian doesn't spend much of his money on anything in his house, but he didn't scrimp on this bed. It has the thickest mattress, the silkiest sheets, and the fluffiest pillow I've ever laid on. It makes it impossible to get out of bed. Even more impossible when my body feels like it's gotten repeatedly hit by a truck.

Caspian spent most of his time away since he gave me his proclamation weeks ago. Most likely because he has a fancy house elsewhere, he enjoys staying at. But even this tiny cabin is beginning to grow on me. I might even fall in love with the simplicity of it, if it wasn't just another form of a prison.

The forest surrounds the cabin on one side, with a small vineyard on the other. Nothing to hear but birds chirping for miles when I sit out on the small deck overlooking the forest and vineyard. But I can understand, if he has a larger, more extravagant house, why he spends most of his time there instead of here.

I don't know what to think about Caspian. We spent a lot of time together the first day when he rescued me, but we haven't spent any time together since. Michi takes care of my every need. He brings me food. It started out simple, just a broth or soup, but now he feeds me more extravagant meals like pasta and meats, both have put some much-needed fat on my bones.

Michi brings me clothes. The small closet now contains almost half as many clothes for me as it does for Caspian.

And he brings me pain medications when I can't take the pain in my legs any longer.

Most of the bruising and swelling is gone. If I wear pants and long sleeves, no one would realize what I have been through. And my leg has healed, mostly. I can walk, but I have a limp. Michi brought me a cane, and that makes walking more comfortable. But I don't want to be using a cane the rest of my life.

It's only been a few weeks, I tell myself. My leg will continue to heal. Even without a doctor.

My month is almost up, and I have no idea what awaits me when my time is up. More importantly, I don't know how to escape. I've tried not to obsess about escaping as I did with Dante. It made it so much harder when I realized I would never escape on my own.

I haven't found a phone or a computer. I have no way to contact Matteo or Arlo, but surely they are looking for me by now. They have limitless resources. They will find me. I just need to give them more time. And in the meantime, pretend I'm in a quiet spa. That's all this is. A peaceful, secluded spa where I heal, uninterrupted.

I hear a door shut, and I quiver. I can never get used to the loud unexpected sounds. Michi is good about trying to be quiet.

I don't know how he lives here by himself in the silence. It's nice for a while, but I'm not sure I could live here indefinitely.

I hold my breath and pull the covers up tighter against my chest. I'm wearing yoga pants and a tank top, but I need more protection against whatever is lurking in the hallway.

Caspian is here. He's only come home a handful of times since I've been here. And he's usually pissed. He yells and stomps like he needs a break from the world and uses this place as his escape.

As long as he doesn't use me as an escape.

He treads heavily through the house, not hiding his anger, while I can barely breathe. All I can do is focus on his footsteps and hope they stay away from this bedroom.

They grow closer, and my heart is in my throat. Caspian may have been nothing but sweet to me when he stole me, but that doesn't mean he will continue to be kind to me. He belongs in Dante's fucked up world. I know what that means. I know what he meant when he said he would break me when Dante didn't.

Caspian is better looking than Dante. Caspian has a charm Dante doesn't. Caspian has a sadness I can connect with. Caspian will still rape me, but when he does, I will make excuses for him. I will want him because sex with him will be better than Dante. I'll fall for him in the same way Beauty fell in love with the Beast. But unlike the Beast, Caspian won't turn into a prince.

Caspian's footsteps get louder, until I know he is pacing outside my door, trying to decide if he will keep his promise to me or not. He's pissed and probably wants a release. He promised he wouldn't touch me for another week, but his reserve seems to be slipping. Whatever happened today has pushed him over the edge.

It wouldn't matter if he broke his promise. I don't get anything if he breaks. I just lose my ability to trust him. Not that I believe him anyway.

I can't do anything but wait and grip the sheets to my chest like holding on and sinking heavy into this bed will save me.

I wait for him to burst through the door and beat me.

He doesn't.

I wait for him to rip off my clothes.

He doesn't.

I wait for him to thrust his cock into my unwilling cunt.

He doesn't.

Nothing happens. I don't know why he made the promise not to touch me for a month. Maybe he was testing his ability to control his urges. Or maybe, he's breaking down my walls so it will be easier to hurt me when he finally does touch me.

Either way, it doesn't matter. He won't touch me. I know that now. Even though he's still pacing, his steps have slowed. He's calmed down. He won't break his promise.

Slowly the door opens, and Caspian enters.

His shirt sleeves are rolled up haphazardly. His blue tie hangs loosely around his neck, and the first few buttons of his once crisp white shirt are undone. There is a hint of red on his shirt, not enough to be blood. Or is it?

I continue my scrutinization of his body. His pants are slightly wrinkled from wearing them too long. And his body hunches slightly, like he doesn't even have the strength to stand upright anymore.

His hair is disheveled. He usually styles his hair in a purposefully tousled way. He's got the perfect bed hair down. But this is more. It's not styled. Just messy. It matches the chaos in his eyes.

He looks like a disaster, but despite whatever he went through to make him look like this, his mouth and body don't give away any distress.

He hasn't said anything since entering the room. He puts his hands in his pockets, most likely to remind himself he can't touch me.

I let go of the sheets and toss them down to my waist. Caspian both scares me and electrifies me. His eyes travel to my breasts, and I ache for more. I see the promise in his eyes, that he will do more if I say the word.

I don't.

I won't give in to his steamy stare. He saved me, but I'm still not free. I will never let a man touch me again until I'm free.

"What happened?" I ask, after several minutes pass of nothing.

He stares, and I see everything. It was bad. Blood everywhere. But he's used to seeing blood and death. The same as me. He lost someone. Not a close relative or friend, but someone he was responsible for. He never fails.

I see it all in his eyes. I'm used to not being able to read people, but Caspian reads like an open book. I'm not sure if I'm not usually observant, or if I prefer not to know. Because if I were able to read the people in my life, I wouldn't like what I found.

Caspian doesn't answer, except with his eyes.

"What do you want with me, Caspian? Let me go. Let me call my family."

He doesn't answer. He stares at me. His jaw eventually ticks familiarly. He does it to hide his real emotions. Because he doesn't want people to know what he's feeling. But I notice.

"Seven more days," he says.

I stare at him, trying to decipher the meaning of his words. He'll let me go in seven days, or he can finally touch me in seven days? He doesn't clarify.

"What do you want with me, Caspian?" I half whisper, half scream.

I expect a smirk or a half-hearted grin. I expect him to think of some deliciously, naughty thing he wants to do to me that I only get a hint of in his eyes.

I get none.

His mind doesn't leave the room. His thoughts stay in the present. And his quietness scares me more than any dirty thoughts ever could.

"Nothing, I should have never taken you," he says so quietly, I'm not sure he said it.

Caspian turns and walks out, leaving me alone with my thoughts. I will never admit my thoughts turn dirty when it comes to him. That Caspian stars in my fantasies. It's just because I've been without a man for so long. It has nothing to do with the man, and it has everything to do with me.

––––––––

One day left.

Days left in my month is how I keep track of time. It's better than counting seconds, like I was doing before at Dante's.

My body wants to spend the day in bed. It's so comfy, and even though I've healed tremendously in the last month, I still have a long ways to go. Another day in bed would do my body good.

I won't lie around my last day though. I need to get up and out. I need to enjoy my last day, if it is, in fact, my last day of 'freedom.'

I stretch, before moving to the edge of the bed. I'm wearing pajama pants and a tank top. I consider changing, but I'm not allowed out of the house except to sit out on the deck, so there is no reason to change. I brush my teeth and comb my hair, which finally has all the knots out of it. And then I walk to the kitchen, smelling the delicious french toast cooking on the stove.

I pour myself a cup of coffee, before Michi realizes I'm awake.

"Wow, I wasn't sure you knew how to get out of bed for breakfast," Michi says.

I smile softly as I lift the coffee to my lips. I don't know what Michi does to the coffee but every time is different and mouth-watering.

I take a sip. "Mmmhmm."

Michi lifts an eyebrow as he holds a spatula in his hand to flip the toast.

"Good?"

I nod. "Delicious as always. Where is this roast from?"

"Hawaii. I thought you deserved a bit of a vacation. And since you can't go to Hawaii, I thought I would bring a tiny part of Hawaii to you."

"Thank you. Is that french toast?" I ask with too much excitement in my eyes and voice.

He nods. "Your favorite."

I bite my lip. French toast was never my favorite. It's always too sweet. But anything Michi makes has quickly become my favorite.

I glance out at the sunlight covering the deck. I want to eat outside, but I want to talk more with Michi first. I glance around the small house and open my ears as best I can, trying to hear if Caspian is here.

"Caspian is at work; you have the house to yourself," Michi says.

I stare up at him incredulously. He can read my mind as easily as I can read the word on the side of the coffee cup.

Buona giornata; "have a good day" in Italian.

I warm. I will have a good day, whatever awaits me. It will be good.

"I put a copy of *Treasure Island* out on the deck for you to read."

"Thank you." Michi has gotten me countless books since I've been here. They are always amazing. Books about adventure or travel. Never about love or family. He's careful with the books he chooses for me. He makes sure they are enjoyable, without reminding me of anyone I might miss.

I drink more of my coffee while Michi cooks. I usually eat my breakfast in bed, and then come out and talk to him for lunch. We never talk about anything serious. He takes my mind away from my life, but I'm running out of time if I want to know anything about Caspian.

"What is it like to work for Caspian?" I ask. I rarely even say his name in front of Michi, so it's weird to say it now.

"He's a good employer. I'm happy, and he's more than generous."

"You live here all the time?"

He nods. "I like the seclusion. I've only taken a handful of vacations in the five years I've worked for him."

"Are you allowed to leave?"

He chuckles with his back to me as he flips my french toast. He finally turns back. "Of course I can leave, Gia. I'm not a slave. How do you think I get this tasty coffee and french toast for you?"

I blush. "What can you tell me about Caspian? How did he get into the security world? Does he date? Does he have any family nearby?"

Michi freezes. "I don't think I should talk about Caspian's personal life. Any questions you have about Caspian need to go to him."

I frown, but I was expecting he wouldn't say much about Caspian Conti. The man will remain a mystery to me, for at least another twenty-four hours.

"Why don't you take your coffee outside and enjoy the sunshine?" Michi says, dismissing me. I don't ask him if he also knows today is my last day of 'freedom,' but it appears from the sadness in his eyes, he knows.

I take my coffee and walk outside to my favorite chair, but it feels more like I'm walking to the guillotine. Or at least my last meal before death finds me.

I don't know what tomorrow brings, but I won't dwell on it. I'll eat my yummy food. I'll read my book. I'll tan in the sun. And I won't think about tomorrow.

My breakfast and lunch are delicious. Michi is an excellent cook. I don't know why Caspian doesn't have him cook wherever Caspian stays when he isn't here.

I hear shouting, and my heart does its usual freeze. I hear Caspian's voice, but I also hear the faintness of a woman's voice.

A woman?

That can't be. Why would Caspian have a woman here?

He wouldn't want to bring a date to see me. I glance at the large glass door out of the corner of my eye, and I can see Caspian standing in the living room as a woman sits on the couch.

What the hell?

I don't move, afraid the couple might notice I'm outside. So far the pair seems to be locked in an argument.

I can't hear the exact words they are saying to each other. But they are yelling.

I turn my head more fully to watch them, not caring if they notice I'm watching. They shouldn't be here if they didn't want me to snoop.

That's when I get my first look at the woman. She's wearing regular clothes. Jeans and a black T-shirt. But her face is puffy from crying. Her auburn hair is matted. And then I see the bruise on the back of her arm.

She was taken, just like me. I don't know if Caspian saved her, the same as me, or if he was the one who stole her in the first place.

Could he not wait one more day to have me? Did he need a release today, and that's why he stole this woman?

Oh, God. I can't be responsible for Caspian hurting another woman. Before I realize what I'm doing, I'm off my chair. I'm at the glass doors trying to listen to the conversation, but the doors are extra thick. I'd guess even bulletproof, and definitely soundproof.

Caspian grabs the woman's arm over the bruise, and I wince, feeling the pain in my own arm. He starts pulling her down the hallway to the bedroom. I can't let him rape her. I can't.

I jerk the door open and shout. "Stop!"

Both of them freeze and stare at me. The woman's eyes are huge, as she realizes Caspian has another woman here. She looks at me like I might be able to free her, but she doesn't realize I am just as much a slave as she is.

Caspian looks at me with rage expanding from his eyes. It's clear he forgot I was even here. And now that I've interrupted, he's even more pissed.

"Stop? What are you going to do to make me stop?" Caspian asks, his voice void of any emotion.

"Please, don't. You promised you wouldn't hurt me for one month. My time isn't up yet, and this would hurt me." I don't think this falls under the rules of our agreement, but I have to try.

He shakes his head. "That's not how our deal works."

I swallow hard, trying to push any fear down. "Please, don't rape her."

The woman's eyes grow larger at my words. But Caspian holds up a hand to silence her. She goes silent, before a word can leave her gaping mouth.

"What does it matter to you if I raped this woman? I promised you a month, and you have one day left. This woman is nothing to you. If she satisfies me, you might even get longer than a month to be free of me."

My eyes cut from Caspian to the woman. I see the fear I've felt too many times. And I see Caspian's rage. I don't think I've ever seen him this pissed before. I've seen a similar look in Dante's eyes. He will beat her within a second of life. Only then, when she has no fight left, will he use his cock to finish her. She will be dead by morning. At least her spirit will. Her body will follow quickly.

"Please?" I say in barely a whisper.

"Why should I?"

Caspian stares at me, not letting me have a moment alone with my thoughts. I can't think. I will do anything to prevent him from hurting her. I can't protect myself, but I can protect her.

"Rape me instead."

9
____

GIA

WHY DID I just tell Caspian to rape me?

Because I can't help myself. I can't watch another woman deal with even a drop of the violation and pain I've felt. I won't let Caspian hurt this woman.

I don't know who she is. I shouldn't feel guilty for any pain she might endure. I shouldn't feel responsible for saving her from the same fate I've faced. But the way her dark eyes bulge wide when she stares at me, with a sadness I didn't think was possible until I was taken, made me want to do anything to save this woman.

I don't care what happens to me. This woman is fragile. She couldn't survive the same things I've been through. She's too kind. One crack of a whip would break her.

Caspian lets go of, and ignores, the woman, as they both stare across the living room at me: his new prize.

I haven't moved since I pleaded with him to take me, instead of her. He hasn't either. We are both locked in a staring contest which might never end. The intensity flowing between us has us locked together in a wind that will never stop blowing.

Neither of us realizes it, but Caspian starts walking toward me. His feet stop automatically, just in time to prevent his body from crashing into mine. God, his eyes are so beautiful. And dangerous. And kind. And mysterious. And bright, but with specks of dark.

I don't breathe. I don't move. I don't back down. I try to lock down everything I'm feeling tight away in my chest so Caspian won't have a clue how to break me, while I try to figure out what he's feeling. He's a walking contradiction. He has equal parts light and dark. But that can't be true. He has to have one side of him that is stronger. Is it the light or the dark?

Right now, dark.

His chest rises and falls sharply as he sucks in all the oxygen in the room with each breath before exhaling deeply enough to blow me over. The beauty I saw on his face turns to a painful stare. All the light from his eyes evaporates until I'm not even sure his eyes are blue anymore.

He's decided. He'll take me instead of the woman behind him. He wants me. And I'm giving myself to him willingly. He doesn't have to tell me his decision. His body does.

I smile. It will probably be my last smile. So I savor it. I let the tiny bit of joy from winning cascade through my body, warming me all the way to my fingertips. My cheeks pink and my eyes soften. I saved her. I don't know who she is, the woman still standing behind Caspian, staring at us like she doesn't have a clue what's happening.

You're safe, I whisper in my head. Run. Hide. Find joy in your last days. I'm not playing games though. I'm not that type of woman. I prefer reality.

"I'll be in the bedroom," I say, turning. Happy to get one more word in before Caspian lets his inner demon out. I can see the evil in him growing stronger and stronger as every second ticks by. Dante lets his monster out freely. Caspian keeps his locked away. It's how he has so much control.

But now I'm permitting him to let his true self out. And it appears it takes Caspian time to unlock the door to the dungeon in his soul. I'm not going to stand here and watch the darkness cloud him, as fear starts creeping up my own body. Caspian doesn't get to see my fear.

My instinct is to wrap my arms around my body as I walk back. Holding myself to bring me comfort and keep Caspian's negative energy away. But I won't let him see me cower. So I strut with my hands by my side. My legs are steadier than they've been since I arrived here.

I open the door to his bedroom. I don't know whether to hope he will follow me immediately, or he will take his time. Immediately, I decide, before I lose my nerve. I want this over fast.

I get my wish.

Caspian presses my body against the wall before I even realize he's in the room. I don't know how he's able to walk in this house without making loud steps.

I wait for the hit. Or for him to choke me. Knock me out again, like he did last time. Or like Dante has done countless times.

I know Caspian is a brute. I see it fully in his eyes now as he pants over me. His breathing may be unsteady, but he is perfectly in control of himself.

I close my eyes slowly and deliberately, trying to find a happy place for my mind to go to. I imagine Caspian's deck, where I've read so many books this last month. What was the name of the last book I read? It had a blue cover, I remember, but the title escapes me. It was about a prince going on a grand adventure to save his kingdom. I try to remember the book, but it's easier to remember the feeling of the sun burning my skin. The smell of the pollen scattered over the deck, making me sneeze. The cool breeze is making me shiver in the early morning, before the sun fully rose.

"Open your eyes, Gia," Caspian says.

I won't. I don't care what he does to me, but I need my happy place. I need to go somewhere that isn't reality. It's the only way I've survived this long.

"Open your eyes, Gia, or I'll go back and—"

I open my eyes. He doesn't have to finish that sentence. I don't want him to hurt that woman. He knows it. And now I've obeyed him, he knows he can use it to get me to do almost anything.

I hate him. Maybe even more than Dante. I could deal with the physical pain as long as I had my escape. I don't know if I can daydream with my eyes open. I need to get under Caspian's skin, so he'll punch me. If my eyes are swollen shut, then he can't ask me to open them.

Caspian shakes his head slowly, side to side.

"You, Gia Carini, made a big mistake."

I swallow hard. I don't disagree. If I cared only about myself, then it was a mistake.

I saved her, I repeat to myself. That's what I need to hold onto. *I saved another woman.*

"You want me to rape you?" he asks, his voice deep and rumbling in his throat.

"Yes," I say, without hesitation or fear.

"Good."

I blink, but force my eyes back open, before the blink turns into shut eyes again.

Caspian licks his lip, like he is deciding the best way to devour me.

And, damn it, my nipples perk up at the thought of his tongue licking me like that.

Caspian will not turn me on. It's just because he's good looking. His body is strong and fit. His hair is luscious and dark. His eyes are what I like most about him, but they've changed. This isn't the same man I had fantasies about. This man is dangerous.

I am not turned on by Caspian, I repeat over and over to myself.

Caspian backs away from my body. He hasn't even touched me yet. Not really. Other than moving me to the wall, but I'm pretty sure my body moved voluntarily.

"Undress me," he says, standing a few feet away from me.

"What?" I ask, not expecting him to give me a command. Dante commanded, but he preferred to use his fists to get me to do what he wanted.

"Do you need your hearing checked?" he asks.

"Um...no...I just...don't understand." I would have expected him to tell me to undress. Dante always kept his clothes on when he raped me. I'm wearing a T-shirt and sweatpants. Not exactly real clothes, but it at least hides my body.

Caspian sighs. "I'm not a patient man, Miss Carini. If you'd prefer I use alternative means to persuade you to behave, then I can. If not, I prefer to give you a command, and for you to follow it as soon as I've said it. Understand?" His voice is threatening. He will hurt me if I don't behave as he says, but if I do, he might not beat me. Can I do that? I hate following men's directions. I've dated a few men that thought they could control me in the bedroom and my normal activities. It never worked out for long.

I just healed. I don't really want a broken bone again. Not so soon. Not when I haven't had a chance to run yet.

And he's asking me to remove his clothes, not mine. He's not asking me to suck his dick or fuck him, yet. I'll behave, as long as it's what I want. Then, I will fight.

I walk over to Caspian. He's wearing a buttoned-down shirt and slacks. I grab the top button at the top of his shirt. My hands tremble at little as I grasp the button. *What the hell is wrong with me?*

I take a deep breath, as I slowly undo the first button.

"Today, Miss Carini," Caspian says, eyeing me firmly. I don't know why I'm Miss Carini, instead of Gia. But I like both of my names rolling off his tongue. Either name he calls me sends chills down my arms and warms my core.

I move my fingers faster, but my stupid fingers stumble at every button, unable to get the tiny buttons to move properly. Caspian doesn't scold me again though. I finish the last button and pull the bottom of his shirt out of his pants. Then, I push the shirt off his broad shoulders, as Caspian shrugs out of the shirt.

My jaw unhinges, staring at Caspian's naked torso. Rippling abs cover most of his body, before forming a perfect V that disappears into his pants. I've never seen a more toned body. But the shock is in the tattoo which winds around his body.

It's a thorn from a rose bush. I know it's a rose bush because he has one in his backyard I've stared at for weeks now. But unlike the rosebush in his backyard that is full of flowers, his tattoo has one single flower on his chest, over his heart. I want him to turn around so I can search his back for more flowers, but I know from the pain in his eyes, there are none.

"What does the tattoo mean?" I ask. I don't expect him to answer me, and honestly, I'm not sure I need him to speak to tell me. It's pretty clear he lives a dangerous life with plenty of thorns. I would guess the thorns represent his kills, and the flower is his heart, slowly withering away.

"The thorns are every time I've felt pain. And the flower is the only time I've felt love."

I catch my breath as he speaks. Love. Caspian is capable of love. He's capable of feeling pain. Dante wasn't capable of either.

"I will never love you; remember that."

Goosebumps cover my body, and I shiver. I don't know why his words affect me so. I don't want him to love me. I know him loving me won't help me escape. I will remain trapped in this house forever, if he loves me. And my only hope at feeling happiness would be for me to love him back. I don't want love. Love is just its own form of a prison.

I want freedom. I never realized how wrong I was in thinking I wanted a boyfriend, before Roman sold me. I'm done with guys. I don't need a man. I just need me.

Caspian's eyes drop to his pants, and I know he wants me to continue undressing him, as he requested.

I squat down in front of Caspian, refusing to kneel. It would feel too much like I'm submitting, and I've had Dante's cock shoved down my throat in that position too many times for me to ever voluntarily get in that position again.

I untie his shoes, careful not to look up at him as I do. I don't need to stir any other feelings, whether pleasant or scary, inside me.

When I've untied his shoes, I carefully remove them. I stare at his shoes a second longer, before I realize they aren't designer shoes. In fact, I would bet they didn't even cost him a hundred dollars. They look nice, but anyone who knows fashion wouldn't be fooled.

I toss the shoes aside.

"Careful with those," Caspian snarls.

I chuckle. "Why? The shoes are cheap. You don't spend any of the money you supposedly make."

Caspian grabs my arm and jerks me up. "I asked you to undress me, not comment on the amount of money I do or don't have. I don't have Carini money, that's true, but I wasn't handed money like you were. I earned every penny. How much money have you actually earned?"

I narrow my eyes, and my anger pulses through me. "You

don't think I earned every dollar I was given? I may not have had a traditional job that brought in new money, but I earned every dollar of my inheritance. Being a Carini isn't easy. Especially being a daughter. There was a reason I was so desperate to find a man on my own. I needed a way out. And the only way to leave was by marrying a wealthy man. Even after my father was gone, it didn't change anything. I was still a woman living in a man's world. Seen as nothing but charming arm candy.

"You don't think my leg was the first broken bone I've ever experienced? Those bruises on my face weren't my first either. My father used to call me a whore. And Dante's men, you killed in front of me to try and scare me, are just a few of hundreds of deaths I've seen before. Don't tell me I didn't earn the money I have! I've spilled more blood and tears earning my money than you have."

My body trembles as I speak. Not from fear, but from the passion in which I speak. I've always felt like I was nothing. Not important. I never brought in any money. I never went to college. I have no special skills. But I do know, unlike other heiresses, I've earned everything. And I won't let Caspian take it away from me with a few words.

"My pants," Caspian says after a few seconds pass.

I glare at him as I roughly remove his belt, then undo the button of his pants, before shoving his pants down. Ensuring to scrape my nails against his legs as I push them down.

I cross my arms, taking a step back now that I've finished undressing him, still steaming.

But then I get a glance of his body. His thighs are bigger than both of my legs combined. Muscles meant for hard work. But it's what's between his legs that has all of my attention. His cock is long and thick, pointing directly at me. He wants me.

I should be disgusted by his cock. I've seen enough of them since I was sold to know it doesn't matter how beautiful of a cock the man has, or how gorgeous the man is, I still don't want a dick inside me that I haven't invited in willingly. But his...

I'm drooling thinking about his delicious cock. I want to feel his dick. I want his thighs pounding it inside me. I've dreamed about sex with Conti. I've imagined it, but even in my imaginations, I never thought his body would be this perfect. I try to think back to the last time he raped me, but he never showed me his body then. Maybe if he did, that time would have been more enjoyable.

No. No. No.

Caspian still wants to rape me. He wants to hurt me. Force me to have sex with him. It doesn't matter if I'm attracted to him, this is still wrong.

My body doesn't understand the difference between right and wrong right now. All it knows is that there is an incredibly attractive man with a cock straining to be inside me. My nipples are hard peaks beneath the thin T-shirt that I know Caspian can see. My cheeks are flushed, and my eyes tell him exactly what I want his cock to do.

I wish this were different. I wish I weren't his captive. Then I would be flirting with him, happy to have a one night stand with him. Instead, I'm doing everything I can to make the walls of my pussy clench up tight, instead of dripping with desire to welcome him in.

Caspian smirks.

And my mouth drops. The bastard knows exactly what he's doing. It's why he had me undress him first. He knew I would find him attractive. He knew I would be conflicted.

Fucking bastard.

"Now, it's my turn."

I gasp as his mouth comes down on mine. His hand cradles the back of my neck, and his lips smash into mine. I haven't been kissed since Roman. Dante and the rest slobbered, but those weren't kisses. And before I realize what my traitorous body is doing, I'm kissing him back.

His lips are so soft and sweet. So different than the way the rest of him is behaving. I can't help but moan as we kiss. I've been so deprived of anything that feels like love. I'm desperate to keep the kiss going. My tongue massages his. My lips push hard against his, needing more and more of the kiss. My hands wrap into his thick hair, keeping his mouth against my lips.

But just as I get what I want, he pulls away, stopping the kiss. I'm breathless, but I will never admit I liked the kiss, or want him to do that again. Never.

He doesn't smile, but I see the hint of pleasure on his swollen lips after our kiss. And I can see in his eyes, he knows I'm reacting the same way.

Damn.

I need to gain control again.

How?

"On the bed," Caspian commands.

Think, think, think. I need to follow his command, but I need to do something that also breaks it at the same time. I walk over to the bed, lie down on my stomach with my feet in the air, making it as hard for him as possible to get what he wants. It's not a great plan, but it's all I have at the moment.

Caspian walks over to the edge of the bed. Not even surprised by my tiny bit of rebellion, and flips me over.

"Undress."

I purse my lips. "I undressed you."

"Fine."

He grabs my ankles and pulls me to him. "I don't need you naked to have you."

My legs dangle over the edge of the bed, as he steps between them, before grabbing my neck again and pulling me into a kiss. This kiss has more passion than our first. His teeth nibble on my lip, but not in an excruciating way. I've soaked my panties by the time he's done kissing me. I fall back to the bed. My lips numb with pleasure.

He kneels down in front of me, his mouth attacking my pussy over my sweatpants.

I gasp and grip the comforter. *What the hell?*

I can't think, as he kisses my most sensitive area over my pants. I haven't experienced any pleasure in months. And I groan and moan, far too loudly for what he is doing.

I bite my lip to keep the sounds from coming and tighten my grip on the comforter. *Why is he doing this?*

He's playing with me. Making me enjoy him. It will make me hate myself later for finding any pleasure in this, but I can't help what my body feels.

He stops.

"Now, remove your pants."

I shove my pants down without thinking, my body already begging for his tongue on my pussy.

"Much better, Miss Carini."

He lowers his mouth over the lips between my legs. What I wouldn't give to have a razor to shave. But his tongue stops, just short of tasting me.

"You don't deserve it, Gia. You don't deserve to feel my tongue flick over your clit, or into the deepest trenches of your pussy. You must learn when you follow my directions, you get pleasure; when you don't, pain."

He flips me back over and smacks my bare ass with the palm of his hand.

"Fuck," I cry out, surprised the small amount of pain caused anything to leave my mouth.

The sting spreads, as he smacks my ass again. I yelp, but it doesn't really hurt. It's nothing compared to Dante. Caspian's smacks won't even leave a mark.

I start panting, anticipating the next smack, but he spreads them out, never letting me anticipate his next strike.

He strikes again and then lets his hand slide slowly down my ass to my dripping slit.

"That turns you on, doesn't it, Gia?"

I bite my lip, not wanting to answer him.

He slides two fingers inside me as he moans. "It does, doesn't it?"

"Yes," I barely whisper.

"God, there are so many things I want to do to you, Gia. But I don't want to break you too fast. Fuck waiting for a taste though."

He flips me again, and his mouth is instantly on my cunt. I cry out in pure ecstasy. I've never felt so much pleasure from a man's tongue pushing into me. My body writhes underneath his touch. And my fantasies become a reality. Caspian Conti is making me orgasm. He knows it before I do. His lips curl up as he makes me come.

"Fuck you, Conti," I cry out, as my body trembles my orgasm.

"I will gladly fuck you."

He stands up with an amused expression on his face. He grabs my legs, jerking my body to him.

"I've waited too long for this." His cock rests at my entrance, and for a second, I think he is going to ask me for permission. Ask if I want him to fuck me.

My answer would be yes. I want Caspian Conti to fuck me. After what he just did to my body, I want to know what his cock would feel like. Sex with him would be amazing. Incredible. I know it without even experiencing it. I know my body craves his. I don't understand it. Other than saving me, he's done nothing to earn me. He doesn't get to fuck me without earning it.

"No," I say, as defiantly as I can. I pull myself back on the bed away from his cock.

He cocks his head to the side and his face tenses. He's not used to being disobeyed. He's not used to being defied. And I prepare for a fight that rivals Dante.

But I refuse to be raped again. I will protect the woman that Caspian brought home, but I won't let him violate me. I can't.

He moves to grab my ankles, but I scoot further away.

"No," I say, louder.

He doesn't stop moving. He crawls up onto the bed, as I continue to scoot back. My head turns to the door. Did he lock it? Could I escape? He's much faster than me. But if my adrenaline is running, could I get free?

"Try it," he growls.

My head snaps back to Caspian. Him reading my thoughts is getting really annoying.

"You can't rape me."

He raises an eyebrow, as he climbs further up until his body is over mine. "I can't?"

"No, you can't. You won't. You're better than, Dante. You won't hurt me like that. You just made me come. You aren't cruel," I say, hoping my words are true.

"Am I?"

"Yes, you're kind."

"No, I'm not kind."

I take a deep breath, and all I breathe in is him. His sweat, his cologne, and my cum on his breath. And it drives my womanhood wild.

"You won't rape me," I repeat.

He frowns, and I see in his eyes that he won't. I don't know why. He's raped me before. He might have assaulted other women before. But I know he won't rape me, now.

"No," he finally says, defeated.

"Will you rape the other woman you stole?" I ask.

He chuckles lightly like he knows something I don't. "No."

I frown. His word doesn't give me much confidence.

"Why?"

He lowers his face until it's directly over mine. "I guess you will have to trust me."

He leans back, and his eyes scan my body with hunger. He still wants me, and my body is craving for his touch again. I feel empty, cold. I want to feel the warmth of his body pressed against mine.

My back arches and my breasts graze his chest. One spark changes everything.

I don't know who kisses who, or whose body crashes with the other first, but our lips lock, and I know nothing will stop us this time. This time, I said yes. I will say yes. This isn't rape. This is the best goddamn sex of my life.

Our tongues dance again, both pushing harder into each other's mouths, both needing more. My fingernails dig into his back sharply as his body presses hard against mine. He settles between my legs automatically, his cock resting at my entrance, and then suddenly, he stops.

"No," I say because I don't want him to stop.

Caspian takes it in the same way as I said before. To stop. With pain in his eyes, he slowly inches off my body.

I grab his neck.

"No, I meant..." *Shit, I can't say it.* I can't tell him to fuck me. He's holding me captive. He wants to rape me. *What's wrong with me?*

But I'm not thinking with my brain. My body is trembling with need for a release. I've been raped, but I haven't had sex. The kind that makes your toes curl, and your body whole. Not in months. I need it. I need it to make all the horrible memories go away. I need it to be my choice. I need to tell him what I want.

He hesitates, not sure what I'm about to say.

"Fuck me, Conti."

His cock slides inside me the second the words leave my mouth. I'm soaking wet, so his passage inside me is easy. But I still stretch around him, as he pushes further in sweet agony.

But the second he does, memories come back. Of him raping me before; of Dante.

"I got you," Conti says. His lips come over my hardened nipple, a move that was only met with rough teeth before, and I calm.

My body comes alive then, pushing out any stray memories. Caspian may have raped me before, but Conti hasn't. Conti was my savior. Conti is who I want to fuck. I want this.

So I don't let the twisted-ness of the situation ruin how I feel.

I arch my back as Conti kisses down my neck, like I had imagined so many times before.

I moan loudly when his cock brushes against a spot deep inside me. A spot no man has ever hit before.

"Yes," I cry, as he hits my clit over and over with his body.

His lips cover mine, silencing me. But my purring continues with his every movement. I can't get enough. My body can't take much more, and yet I want this to never stop. I've never had sex that made me lose my mind like this.

I no longer care about anything terrible Caspian has done before.

I don't care he didn't save me when I ran into his lap from the car.

I don't care he killed a dozen men in front of me.

I don't care he raped me.

I don't care he's holding me captive now.

I'm sick. Sex with him has changed me, and I don't know what to do with myself now.

"Come," he says in a deep, commanding voice. A voice I'm not sure I hate or love. But even if I wanted to disobey his command, there is no way my body could disobey.

"Yes, Conti." I come, screaming his name. Pretending I didn't just let a man who raped me, fuck me.

We both finish, completely spent, but nowhere near sated. The exhaustion gets the best of us, however. We don't talk. We don't fuck again. We drift slowly off to sleep with our arms and legs entangled together.

I realize nothing I thought about Caspian was true. Everything has changed. He's not who I thought he was. *Or he is.* Maybe he is exactly who I thought he is.

10
____

CASPIAN

"No!"

"No, No, No."

"No!"

I don't know who's screaming. *Is it me?* No, I'm not screaming. I open my eyes and feel the wetness on my face. I'm crying from another nightmare. Another reliving of the worst day of my life over and over again.

But with my eyes open, the screaming continues. I turn to my left and see a naked woman flailing next to me, screaming 'no' over and over again. It takes me a minute to realize who the woman is in my arms. I haven't had a woman in my bed in years. At least none whom I allow to stay after the fucking is over.

Gia, I finally realize. I remember. *The sex. God, the fucking sex.* What I did to deserve such a beautifully strong woman, I don't know.

Last night started as a disaster. I considered raping her. That's not who I am, but that's how desperate I was to fuck her. I would do anything, including turn into the type of man I hate, to have her.

She told me, no, and my heart broke. I didn't even realize I had any of my heart left capable of breaking. But then she grew deviant. And I could tell from the gaze in her eyes, she was as torn inside as I was. She wanted me to fuck her, and when she finally said yes, I lost my damn mind.

I only fucked her once, but I already can't imagine fucking any other woman. I loved her mix of strength and sweetness. She fought me every step of the way but then gave into my commands with some persuasion.

Gia isn't my type. I like obedient woman. Women who do exactly what I say without arguing. I like women who don't have a clue what I'm thinking, but Gia seems to guess my every thought.

"Gia," I whisper, afraid if I wake her too abruptly, I'll end up with a broken face or something.

She stirs but doesn't wake.

"No! Please don't..." her voice gets quieter as tears drip down her cheeks.

"Gia, it's okay." I put my arms around her, strategically trying to calm her while ensuring her flailing arms don't find me as a target.

"No! Conti, don't rape me!"

I let go of her when she says my name, and I get smacked in the face by one of her thrashing arms. I don't feel the impact though. I'm too shocked by what she just said. Is she having a dream about last night, when I almost raped her? I didn't, but am I now a bigger nightmare than Dante is to her?

I deserve to be. I'm no better than him. I have different desires than him, but I'm just as capable of permanently scarring her.

Gia's eyes slowly flicker open. They are soaked with her tears. And she cautiously looks around like she doesn't know where she is. I sit on the edge of the bed, staring at her like she's a tiger that made its way into my bed. And if I get too close, I will get clawed.

"Caspian? What are you doing in here?" she asks, moving her body up as she leans against the headboard. She's completely naked, lying on top of the covers, but she doesn't seem to care. I guess weeks of being naked in Dante's world would make her not care.

"We must have fallen asleep after I fucked your brains out," I say.

She blushes, and a slow grin creeps up on her tearstained cheeks.

"Oh, I remember now," she says, smiling like a silly teenager.

"What was your nightmare about?" I ask.

Her smile drops in an instant and small lines form around her eyes, thinking too hard.

"You," she finally says.

I nod. "I thought so. You said my name. Was what happened yesterday that bad, you had a nightmare about it?"

She cocks her head to her side and opens her eyes wide like I'm crazy. Her hand drums up and down her smooth stomach while she waits for me to realize my mistake. I have no idea what mistake I could have made.

"What aren't you telling me?" I feel anger again. She doesn't have to tell me anything, but I want to know everything. I want her to trust me with her everything. I haven't earned it, but that is what I'm used to. We will have to talk later.

"I didn't have a nightmare about last night. Last night was well...last night was pretty great. I had a nightmare about when you came to Dante's."

I frown, not understanding. "I thought when I killed those men in front of you, I didn't upset you?"

"You didn't."

"Then, what the hell are you talking about? The only time

I've been to Dante's in the last month was to kill his men and install the security system. I didn't see you when I installed the security system."

"I'm talking about when you fucking raped me, you asshole!"

Tears, so many tears, flow down her cheeks. She's pissed and angry and hurt. But I still don't have a damn clue what she's talking about.

I can't stand women crying. It might be one of my biggest weaknesses. I reach my thumb up to her cheek, to brush the tears away, so I can focus on this psychotic conversation, but she slaps my hand away.

"Don't touch me."

I jerk my hand back and rub my neck, while staring at her, forcing my eyes to stay on her face instead of perky breasts like my cock wants.

"I don't understand. I've never raped you, Gia. I think I would remember raping a woman like you. The only time I've fucked you was last night."

"No, you raped me. It was one of the worst ones," her voice trembles as she speaks.

"Tell me," I say, hoping her telling me her nightmare, which is most likely just that: a nightmare she dreamed up.

"Dante said he had a surprise for me. Five of his closest friends he owed. Each would get a turn with me. You were first."

She stops, pausing as her eyes shut. She's remembering. And it chills my heart knowing her words are true, even if I'm not the one who committed the crime.

"I was on the bed, spread wide for you. I was cold and warm at the same time. You looked so calm and collected. You wanted me, and I would have given myself to you if you asked. You had saved me."

I bite my lip. Her story can't be true if I had already saved her.

She grasps the end of her long dark hair and twists the strands together in her fingers. "You were my fantasy. My last hope at freedom. When I ran into you that day in the street, I thought you were hot. And somehow your face and body were what I imagined every day when Dante was fucking me. Any chance I could, I pretended he was you. I dreamed about fucking you, instead of him. I fantasized about you coming to save me."

She sucks in a breath that rattles in her throat through her shaky tears. "But then you were there. You were as bad as Dante. You weren't my savior anymore. You wanted to rape me."

"Gia, I—"

"No, let me finish."

I close my mouth.

"You settled your body between my wide, open legs. I couldn't move, I was so badly beaten. You kicked me rougher than Dante ever had. And then, just before you entered me, you realized you couldn't have me watch. You couldn't let me watch you hurt me. So you knocked me out."

I bite my lip to keep from talking. This is her time to talk, not mine. I will have a chance to tell my story.

"And as I was slipping into unconsciousness, you started raping me. I didn't even wake up until after the four other men had violated me. The only way I even knew that it had happened was because of the soreness and cum that kept dripping out of me. The additional bruises that my body earned, even though I was knocked out."

The green in her eyes turns red as she spits her words at me. "You may have thought you were compassionate. But not being awake, not being able to fight, not knowing who has violated my body, is worse than knowing. You are nothing but a coward!" Her voice breaks.

I want to hold her, comfort her, but she doesn't want that.

She doesn't need that. She is fully capable of taking care of herself. And me holding her, would only make things worse. But I need the comfort. I have to wait to get it though.

I open my mouth, wanting to say words to make her feel better, but I'm not sure how to start so she will believe me. I'm not sure she will ever believe me.

I decide right now isn't the time to try.

I get up off the bed while she is still shaking with her anger.

I grab her favorite pajama pants and shirt and place it on the bed next to her. I walk over to my dresser and put on some boxer shorts and sweatpants.

"What do you want for breakfast?"

She doesn't answer. Just stares at me with a gaping mouth at my balls to ask if she wants breakfast when I haven't addressed her story. But I can't tell my side of the story. Not without a lot of help.

"I know you like french toast and eggs. I'll make that and some coffee. Join me out on the balcony when you are ready."

I don't wait for her to answer or yell at me. I walk out and head to the kitchen.

Michi jumps to attention when he sees me. "I haven't started the coffee yet, because I wasn't sure when you'd awake. What should I make for breakfast?"

"Take the day off, Michi."

"Sir, I would be happy to make you breakfast. I don't need a day off—"

I take a deep breath before speaking so that I don't take all my anger and frustration out on him. "Take the day off, Michi. I am fully capable of making breakfast today, and you haven't had a day off in months."

Michi stares at me a moment. I don't think I've ever asked him to take a day off. He's taken only a handful in all our years together. He's like a father to me. He would do anything for me.

And I know he sees the pain in my eyes right now. He wants to help me. But I won't let him.

Michi finally nods and then leaves me alone in the kitchen. I make coffee, french toast, and eggs. I pile everything up on plates and carry it outside. Gia hasn't left the bedroom yet, and I don't know if she's going to or not. But this is the only way to earn her trust.

I set the plates down at the table and then take one of the seats.

The french doors open and Adela steps outside. "Did you make some for me too?"

My lips thin. I want to talk to my sister, but I also want Gia out here. I nod, and Adela takes one of the seats behind a mound of french toast.

Adela takes several bites of her breakfast while studying me. "I guess you aren't going to tell me what last night and this morning was all about?"

I shake my head. "You will find out soon enough."

She shrugs. And I know she already knows more than she is letting on. The walls in my house are thin, so she probably heard plenty of our conversations. And she is more skilled than I am at finding information when she puts her skills to use.

I sit silently, watching Adela shovel in her breakfast.

"You've gotten better at cooking, bro. This is almost edible."

I glare at her. "You seem to be eating it just fine. My cooking is as good as Michi's."

She laughs. "No, it isn't. You aren't the best at everything."

I roll my eyes. I am the best at everything, but I'm not going to argue with my sister about it.

The door slowly cracks open behind me, and my heart stills. *Gia.*

I know without turning my head that it's her. The only other person it could be is Michi, and he knows better than to come back after I gave him time off.

Gia walks toward us. Her feet loud on the deck floor, it creaking below her steps, and then she takes a seat next to me, across from Adela, at the table.

"I'll let you two talk," Adela says, winking at me.

"Stay," I say.

Adela raises an eyebrow, but she eases back into her chair.

I put a plate of food in front of Gia. "Eat. Then, we will talk."

I want her fed before I speak and she storms out without eating. Dante left her far too skinny.

She rolls her eyes at me. "No, talk."

"No, not until you eat."

She pouts, sticking her bottom lip out roughly toward me.

"I'll eat while you talk."

I sigh. "Fine."

I wait until she has eaten a couple of good bites, and then I start.

"Gia, this is Adela, my sister," I say, gesturing toward Adela.

Adela jumps in, like the good sister she is, and holds out her hand. "It's so nice to meet you, Gia. You are such an amazing woman, and I've heard so many great things about you. I've always wanted a sister. I know you aren't exactly my sister, but I hope you don't date this guy," she says, pointing her thumb at me. "He's a bit of an asshole, but you already know that. I'm just so happy to see a woman in his life at all."

Adela speaks without taking a breath. But Gia smiles as she shakes her hand.

"It's very nice to meet you too, Adela."

Gia lets go of Adela's hand and turns to me with an evil grin on her face. She slaps me hard across the jaw.

"You are worse than an asshole. You are a motherfucking

jerk-bastard-man who deserves to get shot repeatedly in the leg every few weeks, just after you heal."

I nod. "Jerk-bastard-man?" I smile a little at her new nickname for me.

"Yes, that's what I said, and I stand by it."

She crosses her arms. "I can't fucking believe you. You led me to believe you were going to hurt her. She's your sister! I know you are a bastard, but I don't think you would ever rape your sister."

Adela eyes me suspiciously.

"Really, Adela?"

She laughs. "No, I don't have to worry about that. You would never rape any woman." Adela glances between Gia and me, her smile faltering. "Wait! Did you rape Gia?"

I turn from Adela to Gia. "That's what we need your help with Adela."

"What? Did you rape her last night?"

"No," Gia and I both say in unison.

Adela visibly relaxes in her chair, her body sinking into the wicker and cushions. "Thank God! If I had thought you would have actually have raped her last night, I would have never left you alone with her."

I shift my weight in my chair, not letting her know I almost did rape Gia. But Gia again saved herself. I'm not as good of a person as Adela thinks I am. I don't deserve any of the affection Adela gives me.

"How can I help then?" Adela asks.

"Where was I last Tuesday?"

Adela narrows her eyes. "What time?"

"Three PM."

"You were running on the boring ass treadmill at the gym, twenty minutes from here on Ratonni street."

"How about last Sunday at ten AM?"

"You were installing a security system in Milan."

"And how about three Saturdays ago at six PM?"

"You were getting a manicure."

Gia laughs at that.

"Adela has a photographic memory. Everything she reads, sees, or hears, she remembers. It's quite annoying, actually." I give a dirty look to Adela, who laughs at me.

"It's true; I remember everything. My husband, Rodolfo, hates it. He never wins a fight."

Gia continues her careful laughing.

"And how do you know everything about my schedule and daily life?"

"Because it's my job to know. I protect you. I work for you and so most of the time I'm with you, and when I'm not, I have access to all of the security. It's my job to keep you safe."

I turn to Gia. "Satisfied she knows my whereabouts at all times?"

Gia nods slowly.

"Eat," I command, looking at her still full plate.

Gia lifts her fork and cuts off a bit, before sticking a bite in her mouth.

"Tell Gia every time I was at Dante's house while she was captive there."

"The first time was Tuesday, the second of May. You were there to install the security system. I was with you the entire time. I don't trust Dante, and I thought he might try to backstab us. As soon as the system was installed, I was able to monitor every part of the house. Including you Gia..."

Adela's voice grows sad when she says she could see Gia. I've watched enough of the security feed of what Dante did to Gia to want to go over and strangle him with my bare hands, bring him back to life, shoot him, and then bring him back to life again and continue until he can't survive any longer.

"Any other times?" I ask, prodding Adela.

"Yes, the day you rescued Gia."

Gia's mouth falls a little. And I can see her un-chewed food in her mouth. It doesn't make me stop wanting her.

"Do you have any questions for Adela?" I ask Gia.

Gia shakes her head, although I'm sure Gia will eventually have a million questions for Adela.

"Adela, give Gia and me a few minutes alone."

Adela smiles sweetly and nods. "Of course." Adela gets up and walks over to Gia, squeezing her in a comforting manner on the shoulder. Then Adela looks at me, and I know she is going to be listening to every word of our conversation. At least Gia doesn't have to know that.

I wait until Adela walks back inside.

"I never raped you, Gia."

She looks up from her plate, staring at me like staring at me is the most important thing in her life. Like her life depends on finding my secrets.

"I believe Adela. I believe she thinks she knows what you do at all times. But she can't possibly know. You could have snuck away for a few minutes that day."

I nod. "I could have."

"So why would I believe you? Why would I believe you when you say you didn't rape me?"

"I'm not asking me to believe me. I'm asking you to believe yourself."

She bites her lip.

"You already know it wasn't me that raped you. You just said it was *pretty great* when I fucked you. Although, I'm sure it was far better than *pretty great*."

She blushes and sits back in her chair like she's trying to hide.

"Do you think if I had raped you, sex with me would have felt that amazing?"

She doesn't answer.

"Do you think you would have wanted to have had sex with me if deep down you truly believed I had raped you?"

Nothing.

"Do you believe I'm capable of raping you?"

She glances back up at me. "No, I don't think you raped me. I don't think you've raped anyone or are capable of rape."

My lips twitch. If she only knew the truth, she wouldn't be saying I'm not capable. But as much as I wanted to, I never touched her without her permission.

"I just can't make sense of what I remember," she says, staring down at her french toast again as she uses her fork to move the food around on her plate before taking a bite.

"Is it possible it was another fantasy? That whoever was hurting you was too much for you? So you changed the image of the man hurting you to me, so it was easier for you to take?"

She nods. "It's possible."

"If you need, Adela can find the security tapes and try to find the tape of the rape you are talking about. If it will help."

She nods. "I'll think about it."

I nod. I'm sure Adela has already scanned the images in her head and found the exact instance Gia told me about earlier.

But it will be tough for Gia to watch. It was impossible for me to watch without punching the display.

Gia finishes every bite of her breakfast, to my surprise. "This is better than Michi's." She pauses. "But don't tell him I said that; he'd be crushed."

I chuckle. "Don't worry, Michi will love you no matter if he finds out you prefer my cooking to his or not."

Gia's eyes warm as she wipes her red lips with a napkin.

"So what now?" she asks.

I raise an eyebrow. "I'm not sure what you mean?"

"When will you let me go? It's clear you aren't the monster you said you are. When will I be free?"

I sigh. "I'm still the monster, Gia. Just not the same monster Dante is. You'll figure out my darkness soon enough."

"When will I be free?"

"Never."

Her hope drops. "Why? Why not just let me go?"

"I can't."

"Why?"

"The why doesn't change what is. You will never be free. So start finding ways to enjoy your life here with Michi, Adela, and me. You enjoy your books. We can get you more and—"

"No, I am not your captive."

I smirk. "It seems like you are."

She crosses her arms stubbornly. "I won't have sex with you again. You will have to rape me." Her voice is defiant, but her eyes are half filled with lust. She can't hold out. She needs sex with me as much as she needs air to breathe.

I lean forward and sweep a hair off her face. She doesn't move, but her eyes fill higher and higher until I know she is imagining me naked.

"I think you can be persuaded."

11

GIA

Caspian is so confusing.

He's sweet and charming. He's menacing and a liar. He's truthful. He's every personality that has ever existed. And it turns me on and pisses me off at the same time. I don't know what's wrong with me. But I can't live like this. I need to know what he wants with me, other than sex. The sex is amazing, but it won't last. He will get bored with me. *So why keep me forever?*

Above everything, he's kinder than he thinks. He's saved me more times then he realizes. I just wish I could break through his control and figure out what's going on in his head. He's so careful with what he tells me I think he could point back to always telling me the truth, but he's clearly hiding something. A lot of things, actually.

There is only one bad thing he's ever really done. Denied me my freedom.

I know now he never raped me. I trust his words. I trust Adela, even though I'm pretty sure I'll want her to show me the video later. I need to know what happened to me when my mind was weakened. But after having sex with Caspian, I know he

135

didn't rape me. That's one line I don't believe he would cross. At least not with me.

I haven't moved from my chair on the balcony after Caspian left. I finished my coffee almost an hour ago, but I can't bring myself to go inside and get another coffee. The warm sun is too cozy to leave, even for a minute. And when I go back inside, it means this is real. I'm his captive. He saved me to make me his.

Forever.

That's the word he used. Forever.

I just have to figure out to change forever to a month. I could use a month longer healing here. Hiding out from Dante where it's safe, and fucking Caspian whenever I get a chance. Then, when the month is up, I could seek my revenge. I'd be strong enough by then, and have Caspian out of my system.

But then what? What life would I go back to? The aunt who doesn't have a life of her own? Who has never had a life of her own? I'll worry about that once I get out of here. First, I need to get Caspian to agree to my plan.

I jump up, now that I have a plan. I can agree to all his darkest sexual fantasies, in agreement for him letting me go in one month. He won't be able to resist. If I'm here any longer than that, I will just become a headache or a liability. At least that's what I convince myself my argument is as I race inside his small cabin.

I listen, trying to hear where he or Adela is. I look down at the couch that is now stretched into a bed where Adela must have slept. But I don't see any other sign of her.

I do smell coffee. I can't resist getting another cup. I assume I will find Michi in the kitchen, but he's gone. Adela or Caspian can't be far away. Someone must have refreshed the coffee recently. I pour myself the steaming liquid gold and then walk through the house.

It takes me all of two minutes to walk through the entire

house. I will never understand why he has such a small house. He must have another house somewhere else. He might even have a family, a wife, children he is hiding from me.

No one is in the house.

I consider my next move. *Could I run?*

My leg is mostly healed. Enough that I could walk, or even jog, for miles. No one is here to stop me.

I know Caspian has a security system. *Is one of his employees watching me right now?*

I sigh.

I'll try running if my plan fails. I'm safe. Caspian won't hurt me. Dante doesn't know I'm here. And I can keep having mind-blowing sex. My life could be worse at the moment.

Still...

I move to the front door and rest my hand on the door handle. *What would happen if I opened the door?*

My pulse raises with anticipation. I bite my lip as I grin. I like playing devil's advocate too much.

I turn the knob, surprised the door even opens. And then I step out on the small porch of the cabin. Nothing happens. No alarms sound. No men come racing out of the bushes to pull me back inside. *Maybe Caspian was lying about the security?*

I sigh. He's not lying. Just not telling the whole truth. He knows I'm out here.

I walk down the three steps and sit on the bottom step, my feet hitting the gravel outside of the house for the first time since I arrived. I sip my coffee and wait.

I don't have to wait long. Five minutes later, maybe, I see Caspian running up the drive. *Shirtless.*

My mouth falls open seeing his rippling muscles contract. I lift my cup of coffee to my mouth to cover my gaping. I glance over at the side of the house and realize his car has been here the whole time. I could have searched for his keys and tried to escape.

He would have found me. I'm sure his car has a GPS system.

I turn back to the gorgeous man sparkling under the sun reflecting off of his glistening skin.

Damn, maybe I should agree to stay for two months. I could stay locked up in this tiny cabin if it meant two months of fucking him.

"You wouldn't be trying to escape, would you?" he asks.

"Nope, just drinking my coffee on the front porch." I take a sip of my coffee to prove my point.

"You don't listen to music when you run?" I ask, noticing he doesn't have any earbuds in.

"No need. I have voices in my head far too often. I prefer to run alone."

I narrow my eyes. "What does that mean?"

Caspian stretches his arms over his head, and my insides are putty. My nipples perk up, thinking they are about to get attention. And my core burns with desire.

He shrugs. "I have earbuds in often to communicate with my security teams. I prefer to be alone when I run."

I nod. That makes sense. But again, I get the feeling that although it's true, it's not the reason he doesn't listen to music.

"I have a proposition for you," I say, letting the previous topic go.

He bends down, stretching at the waist. "So you were trying to escape. Just with propositions this time, instead of running."

I frown. "How do you know what my proposition is about?"

He straightens. "Because I know you. "

I pout. "No, you don't."

He cocks his head to the side. "You're Gia Carini. Third born. You are the child your mother thought would save her marriage to your father. She was wrong.

"You weren't exactly neglected as a child, but you were not praised like your brothers. You never fully belonged in their world. You were just one more child to split the inheritance with.

"You just floated by in school. Never really pushing yourself, but getting mostly A's all the same. You never went to college, didn't even apply. Why would you? You are the beautiful woman your family uses to distract other men when it suits them.

"And then you met a man, Roman. You thought he was different. He could give you a real life. A purpose. So you fell in love, and now you're here. How I'd do?"

I set my coffee cup down on the step before I stand calmly. "Like you had Adela do a background check on me and figure out the basics. That doesn't mean you know me."

He takes a step closer to me, closing the already tiny gap and setting off an electrical pulse. It starts off slow, as his hand grazes my fingertips accidentally, and then races faster as it hits every major nerve in my body.

"You're incredibly stubborn. You won't take no for an answer. You hate to be controlled. You're naïve. You're a bit of a princess who is used to other people taking care of them. Your beauty has gotten you far in life."

I glare at him, hating where he is going with this.

"But you are also an incredibly strong, intelligent, and fierce woman. One that could put me on my knees with one word. That's how I know you what you are about to propose."

He's right. He knows me better than I want him too.

"And that's why I'm not going to stick around and listen to it."

"What?" the word slips out of my mouth more in shock than an actual question. He slips by me, jogging inside.

It takes a second for the shock to wear off and the annoyance to set in. He will too listen to me.

I stomp inside, not even bothering to pick up my coffee mug. I slam the door behind me and then I listen, waiting to figure out where Caspian went.

Shower. I can hear the water on. I smile; the benefits of having a small home.

I take loud steps, making my presence known as I make my way to the bathroom.

Caspian has kicked off his running shoes and is standing in the bathroom with the water running. He sees me, smirks, pushes down his running shorts and flicks them in my direction before stepping into the shower.

I gape for a second as his body disappears behind the glass doors.

"Caspian! You don't get to end a conversation like that!" I yell when I regain my composure.

He ignores me and grabs the bottle of shampoo.

He doesn't get to win without even hearing me out.

I stomp to the shower door and throw it open. "Talk to me, damn it!"

Nothing. He pretends I'm not even here. He massages the cream colored liquid into his hair until it begins to lather.

I don't think. I want him to talk to me, and this is the only way I know how. I rip the clothes off my body and step into the shower.

He continues to ignore that I'm here. Instead, he tilts his head back and closes his eyes as he rinses the shampoo. I stop thinking for a moment while I watch the suds drip down his hard chest.

I shake my head, forcing myself to focus.

"Look at me, Conti!" I yell.

He finally does with an amused expression.

"Yes?"

Damn, I can't think. All I can do is stare at his lips. I forgot how inviting they are. I want him pressed against mine. And then sucking on every sensitive part of my body.

No.

Focus.

"I want to make a deal. You don't want me here forever. I'm a liability. I'll drive you mad. It's clear you are a loner."

He shrugs. But he's listening closely.

"Let me go in two months. I mean, one month. You can have me for one month. Do anything you want. All those dirty thoughts floating around in your head can be a reality. For one month. Then let me go. You don't want the trouble I bring anyway."

He leans forward until his lips brush against mine, the water dripping down his face and rolling onto mine. I shiver.

"No."

My heart stops. He said no, but I don't care about his answer. I care about what I want. I want sex.

My lips close the gap, needing his lips on mine. He doesn't hesitate. He kisses back with the force of the universe pushing us together. I don't understand the attraction between us. It's not like the attraction between Roman and me. This is different. Very, very different. It's all-consuming.

I can't think about escaping when I want to go deeper into his abyss. I want him more and more until I no longer feel like myself except when our lips are locked. I've never felt like myself until now.

I should have learned my lesson. Relying on a guy to make me whole is what landed me in trouble. I was raped and abused because I trusted a man with more than he had earned. But Caspian saved me. He's not evil. And it's just sex.

The sex will eventually get boring. We aren't together. We aren't a couple. Eventually, Caspian will let me go. And then I can find my own life, without a man.

"What do you want, Gia?" he asks as he presses me against the back of the shower. The cold tile presses against my back. He's asking if I still want my freedom. How can I say it's what I want when all I can think about is his body? I'm not sure when I will be ready to give him up. One month won't be long enough. I don't even know if two months would be long enough.

"Freedom, I want freedom. I just don't know how to get it," I whisper.

"I do. Let me take you away from everything." He doesn't wait for me to respond. He kisses down my neck as he palms my breast. I've never had shower sex. Never felt the slick water racing down my face. Never been with a man who is half monster and half angel.

But that is exactly who Caspian is.

My body comes alive under his touch. I forget about everything but him. He's right that it feels a lot like freedom. At least it does in my head, even if my body isn't really free.

His eyes rage with lust as I writhe under his touch.

"You have the body of a princess," he says, lowering how mouth to my nipple to lick the sensitive bud.

I arch my back, needing more of the flickering he's doing with his tongue.

"And the heart of a warrior." He releases his latch and sinks his hand between my legs. He hits my favorite spot without even trying.

I see the look of something darker in his eyes. He wants more than what he's about to do to me. This time is for me. But if I want to win this game we are playing, I will have to give into his desires. Is he as twisted as Dante?

No, but he said he was worse. I still don't know what that means, but I plan on figuring it out.

Right now though, I just need the release of freedom he promised.

His cock pushes into my stomach, and I ache to have him inside me.

But he's patient. As much as my body presses against his, needing to feel his slick length inside me, he won't let me until he says so. He may not seek everything he wants when he's with me, but he still has the control.

"Come, Gia," he commands as his fingers slide inside my slit while his thumb presses the button to build me.

"Conti!" I cry as an orgasm rolls through me.

His eyes blaze as he watches me follow his command. I pant for several seconds, trying to get my hold on reality again.

"How do you do that?" I ask breathing slightly more regularly, but his hand is still buried inside me.

"The question you should be asking is why. Why do I do that when I should be punishing you?"

"But—"

I don't get to speak. His mouth covers mine, taking my voice and any thoughts with me.

His cock replaces his fingers inside me, stretching me to my brink. He pumps quickly in and out of me, not giving either of us time to say anything to each other.

He lifts my legs up, and I dig them into his back as my hand grips his neck, holding on for my life as he moves us faster and faster.

"I can't," I cry, knowing his body is begging me to orgasm again, but there is no way my body can handle that again so soon.

Caspian stills, and strokes my face, running his thumb across my bottom lip. He smiles sweetly, even though his cock is still inside me. There is nothing sweet about Caspian.

"Beautiful," he says simply.

I blush at the simple compliment I wasn't expecting in the midst of quick shower sex.

His sweet smile turns wicked. And then he thrusts. My body clenches around his cock. My soul contracts to the beat of his breathing. And I know I'm going to be lost to Caspian forever.

"Conti!" I cry again, loving the way his name rolls off my tongue.

I hold onto him with everything I have as he slams his body into mine. He's not gentle as his own orgasm takes over him. My body hits the shower tile over and over.

It's hard. It's primal. And it's something that has been missing from my life for a long time: passion.

I clutch onto him knowing I don't know when I will have to let this feeling go, let Caspian go.

"It's Caspian, by the way," he says as he slowly stills, both of our breathing still frantic.

"I like Conti better. Conti saved me from my nightmares."

He frowns. "Conti doesn't exist. You saved yourself."

Jesus, my heart stops. Can Caspian say anything more perfect right now? While at the same time moments ago, say all the wrong things?

It's a good thing my heart is stopped right now, because I don't trust it. If Caspian gave me my freedom right now, I'm not sure I would take it. He treats me well. Then he treats me horrible. He can say the sweetest compliments and the most awful insults. Sex with him is incredible, but also intense. His house is homy but also feels like a prison.

I like Caspian. More than I would ever admit to him or myself. But like isn't love. And even if I loved him, the thought of that feeling got me in trouble before. I can't stay here forever. Whatever this is, needs to end. It would be so much easier if I hated him.

Why don't I hate you, Caspian?

12

―――――

GIA

CASPIAN NEVER SAID yes to my proposal. He also never gave me a definitive no. Neither is surprising. We don't really talk. We fuck.

I'm not complaining. The sex is amazing, but I need to figure out what is going on in Caspian's head to have a chance of getting free.

I woke up this morning without a nightmare. Which means Caspian slept in the bed with me last night. He only has twice. Usually, he sleeps on the couch in the living room. He hasn't said he doesn't like sleeping with me. But I assume it crosses some line in his book. Makes whatever this is, too relationship-y. But I want him in my bed every night. He keeps my demons away.

I put on some jeans and a fitted white shirt that makes my boobs look fantastic. I comb my long hair and then hurry out to see if I can find Caspian before he leaves for work, or wherever he goes when he isn't here.

"He's not here," Adela says, stopping me as I reach the kitchen.

She sits at a barstool eating her breakfast. Michi is in the kitchen cooking omelettes.

I frown as I glance at the clock on the microwave. It's seven

145

in the morning. I didn't exactly sleep in, but I have no idea what time Caspian usually wakes.

She smiles at me. "Don't worry; he didn't run out on you on purpose. He had a meeting. That's why I came over so early: to keep you company."

Adela's voice is strong and happy. She reminds me of myself before life destroyed me.

I don't have the heart to tell her even if he was here this morning; it wouldn't mean we would have some romantic moment. Her eyes seem too hopeful for a relationship that will never happen between us.

"You mean you are here to make sure I don't run away."

I take a seat next to her as Michi pours me a cup of coffee. He's whistling to himself, ignoring my sharp words.

My words don't faze Adela. "I don't need to be here to make sure you don't run. You won't run."

I shake my head. "You Contis underestimate me."

She chuckles. "I don't think Caspian underestimates you at all. I think that's why he's fascinated with you. He doesn't know what to do with you. And I'm not a Conti by the way, so don't group me in with him."

"I thought you were his sister?"

"I am. I'm just married. I'm a Caruso now."

I stare at her in disbelief. I never expected her to be married. To have some resemblance of a normal life.

She smiles. "I've shocked you."

I nod.

"Good, I didn't think that was possible."

"Omelette, okay?" Michi asks.

"Of course."

He places the omelette in front of me. "My cooking may not be as good as Caspian's, but mine is more reliable."

I chuckle. "Caspian told you?"

He gives me a wink. "Yes, I guess I will have to work harder to gain your approval."

"Your food is amazing. It's just—"

"Caspian's is better. You're wrong, but I get it. When you love someone, it's easy to look past their faults."

"I do not love Caspian! He's holding me captive. How could I love someone who took away my freedom?"

Adela sinks in her chair, as her and Michi exchange knowing glances.

Michi shakes his head at me. "Love is strange. You don't get to choose it. It chooses you. I believe you if you don't love him now, just be careful. Love sneaks up on you when you least expect it to."

I take a bite of my omelette. I'm not going to argue with Michi about loving Caspian. It's not possible for me to love a man who took my independence away, my choices away, for even one second.

I turn to Adela as Michi starts cleaning the dishes in the sink.

"You have the security footage of Dante's house?"

She nods slowly, only looking at me out of the corner of her eye as she tries to sip her coffee casually.

"You had a camera in the room where I was kept?"

She nods even slower.

"I need to see. I need to know Caspian never touched me."

She swallows her coffee, hard. "Are you sure?"

"Yes."

She stands and walks slowly toward the front door, like if she walks slowly I might change my mind. She exits, and I think maybe she is leaving, rather than getting the recording. But a few minutes later, she returns with a computer in her hand.

She walks back next to me and opens the computer. She glances at Michi.

"I think I'm going to go for a walk down to town. Get us some nice wine to enjoy with our pasta tonight," he says before walking out the front door.

Adela turns to me. "What do you want to see?"

"The night that five men came."

She nods. She starts typing into the computer searching files, and then she clicks on a video.

She turns the computer back to me. "Do you want me to stay or give you some time?"

"You've already seen it?"

She nods. "I spent most of my time since Dante captured you monitoring you."

"Why?"

"Because Caspian couldn't. He wanted to make sure you were still okay."

My heart hurts. How could he think I was still okay when he knew what Dante was doing to me? How could he wait so long to rescue me?

"It killed Caspian to leave you there. I know he hasn't told you why yet. I've told him he needs to tell you why soon. I don't know if he will, but it's not my place to explain. Just know he had a reason, and it tormented him every hour he left you with that monster."

Her words don't make me think any better of Caspian.

"I don't care if you stay or not." It's the truth. She's already seen the horror. I've experienced it. Watching it can't be worse than feeling it.

I turn the computer toward me so I can have a good view. And then I press play.

"I think I'll stay," Adela says softly, sitting next to me.

I don't look at her. I can't take my eyes off the completely broken version of myself lying in the room.

There is no audio. It's a good thing, because I could probably hear my broken heart beating so weakly, if I weren't sitting here right now I would think the woman on the video was about to die. I would have.

Dante enters with five men on his tail. All look strong and defiant. He makes a joke and they all chuckle as he kicks me hard. That part was real. Then a man with a similar build to Caspian steps forward. The man has a similar build and similar eyes. But this man is skinnier than Caspian. He's weaker. He could pass as a distant cousin of Caspian, but he's not him.

I watch as he kicks me and I feel the ache in my ribs. I watch as I'm dragged to the bed. It's like I'm there, but I'm not. I'm floating in a cloud looking down at my naked and bruised body, helpless to save myself from the fate that awaits me.

I'm tied to the bed. And then the coward settles between my legs before knocking me out. He could see my need for revenge in my eyes. He knew I would come after him if I remembered what he did. So he tried to take away my memories.

But I will never forget his face. Not until I've killed him.

I continue watching. I watch each thrust, each grab of my breasts, each punch to the gut.

A tear escapes my eye as I watch. It's painful and horrible, and exactly what I needed to remember Caspian isn't much better. He wanted to do the same thing to me. He's locking me up, keeping me from seeking my revenge.

My tears turn to flames fanning an invisible fire growing stronger as each second of the video passes. I watch each man climb on top of me and use my body like they use a piece of exercise equipment. Like I'm not human.

Finally, it's Dante's turn, but I don't need to see what he does to me. I remember every second of him.

I close the computer. I'm not sure if I'm stronger or weaker for watching it.

"Stronger," Adela says as I wipe the tears from my cheek on the back of my hand.

"What?" I whisper, my voice hoarse.

"You are strong, Gia. The strongest. No one can take that from you. That's one of the reasons you stayed as long as you did. You were strong. You survived until we could get you out. And you're stronger now."

I smile weakly. "You are definitely a Conti, no matter what your last name is now. I don't know how you guys do it, but you are always able to read my mind."

"I've been watching you for a long time. I have a good idea of what you are thinking."

I nod.

"I need something to drink," I finally say.

She jumps up. "We have wine or whiskey or vodka or..."

"Whiskey."

She fixes an overfilled glass and slides it to me.

"You aren't going to join me?" I ask. It's eight in the morning. It's not surprising that she won't drink with me.

"I would, but I can't."

"Work?"

"No." She pauses. "Can you keep a secret?"

I shrug. "Sometimes."

"I think you will be able to keep this one. I'm pregnant!"

"Congratulations!" I say staring down at the invisible bump under her dark grey T-shirt.

"But why is it a secret?"

"Because if I told Caspian, there is a chance he wouldn't let me work as hard or would put me on desk detail instead of helping him. He's never denied me the ability to do what I love before, but I'm afraid if I tell him I'm pregnant, he won't let me continue working for him. Caspian has always trusted me with my safety. He's let me make my own choices. He knows I can take care of myself and kick anyone's butt when need be. He's never told me I can't before. That's what is so great about our relationship: we are a perfect team working together. He's not my boss. We work together."

I hate it, but I respect Caspian more for treating his sister this way. My brothers were always too protective of me. Never let me do anything without security and protection. I guess they were right to worry because of where I am now, but maybe if I had had the skills Adela has, I wouldn't be here.

"But I'm afraid when Caspian finds out I'm pregnant he won't be able to resist keeping me away from all of this to keep me safe."

"I won't tell Caspian. I promise."

"Thank you. It's so exciting to tell someone. I'm excited to be a mom, but I love working security." Her arms go around me before I realize it.

And I melt in her arms. This is exactly what I needed. A hug from a friend.

Caspian might be dark, but there is nothing but warmth in Adela. She loves her brother, and it's not her fault he has an evil side. I won't fault her for that. She's a friend. I just don't think I can trust her judgment of Caspian.

There is no reason he should have left me with Dante if he could have saved me. If her words are true, there is nothing he could do to ever earn my forgiveness. He might have saved me, but nothing can save him from what he's done.

13

CASPIAN

Today sucks.

Worse than sucks. Today destroyed me.

It knocked me on my ass time and time again. Beat me until I have nothing left. Ripped out the tiny bit of strength I have left, leaving me weak and vulnerable.

I need today to be over. It's gone on far too long. I'll take a fifth of whiskey to my bedroom and drink until I pass out. Tomorrow will be better. It has to be. I know from experience.

It's been five years since I lost my will to live. Each year on the anniversary of my life ending, I think it will get better. I plot my revenge thinking this year it will be different. This year, I will finally kill them all for taking my life from me. But instead, I realize I have a tiny bit of life left in me when another piece of it is taken.

I slam my front door, not caring if I startle Michi. He's used to me coming home angry. He knows not to linger today. He'll be hidden away in his room. I'm sure he made dinner and left it warming in the oven as always, along with a new bottle of whiskey.

I head to the kitchen. I don't care about the food, but I need the whiskey.

I exhale when I see the bottle of whiskey on the counter. If I didn't have the bottle, I wouldn't survive another second. I smell the chicken warming in the oven, but it makes my stomach churn at the thought of food.

I snatch the bottle off the counter as I stomp to my bedroom, loosening my tie as I walk. In a few more minutes, today will be over. I'll have drunk enough to wash my memories into oblivion. And I won't wake until the sun has risen.

I throw my bedroom door open as I kick off my shoes. All I can think about is getting the bottle of whiskey into me as fast as possible. I unscrew the top and lift the smooth bottle to my lips, tilt the bottle up, and begin gulping the liquid, feeling it burn down my throat and welcoming the feeling.

When I lower the bottle though, the pain is still there. I glance at the amount of liquid I drank. Almost a fourth of the bottle. It's going to be a long night if that amount did nothing to make me numb.

I take a step forward and stub my toe on the corner of my bed.

"Fuck," I curse, as I toss the bottle of liquid against the wall without thinking.

The bottle shatters as the liquid sprays everywhere in the dark room.

"Caspian?" a tiny voice asks gently from the bathroom.

I close my eyes and grab my head. I forgot Gia was here. Usually, she is all I think about when I'm working. Her breasts bobbing up and down as I push inside her. Her swollen lips begging for me. Her raspy voice as she comes at my command. I can't get her out of my head on a normal day.

But today is different. Today, Gia didn't even exist.

I can't handle her today. *Not today.*

I should call Adela and have her take Gia to her house. Or tell Michi to take her to a hotel. I need Gia anywhere but here.

I walk to my ensuite. The door is cracked, and the light peeks through the bottom of the door into the dark bedroom. I never bothered to flip the lights on.

I open the door and step from the darkness into the light of the bathroom. Gia is sunk into the tub with bubbles dancing on the surface, hiding her gorgeous body from me. A candle is lit sitting on the ledge near the tub, along with a glass of red wine and a book.

My mind goes back to the first time I bathed her in the tub. And for a split second, I think I want to join her in the tub and then fuck away the dark memories clouding my mind. It won't work though. The memories will remain.

When Gia looks up at me, she doesn't look afraid. Her eyes are big, but more out of concern than fear.

"What happened? I heard a loud crash," she asks her voice calm.

I ignore her question. She doesn't need to know I just threw away my only hope at getting any relief tonight. Hopefully, Michi stocked the liquor cabinet well, and I can find another bottle to drink.

"You need to leave," I say, staring down at her nipples piercing through the bubbles.

She narrows her eyes as she takes the glass of wine off the shelf and brings it to her lips slowly.

"Leave?" she asks calmly.

Her calmness is annoying me. I'm not calm. I know she can feel the rage emanating from me. Her eyes tell me she knows exactly what I'm thinking. She always knows what I'm thinking. It's the weird connection between us I can't understand. Like we've known each other for a lot longer than the few weeks she's been here.

"Yes, leave." I snatch the towel off the hanger and hold it out to her, assuming she will stand and take it from me.

Instead, she flicks her big toe up, playing casually in the bubbles.

"What happened?"

"I need you to leave, Gia. You can sleep in Michi's room. I'll get him a hotel room for tonight. I need you away from me."

She nods, and I think she will agree. "I'll leave after I finish my bath. I just got in. I was planning on soaking for about an hour while I read my book and finish my wine."

"No." I can't handle her defiance. Not even for a second.

"Then, talk. What. Happened?"

"No."

I grab her arm and pull her up, shoving the towel around her body.

"Out. Now." I growl.

She smirks, and her eyes gleam with her defiance. Her dark eyes scan my body looking for a clue to what happened. Her mouth falls open when she finds it.

"Oh my god! You're bleeding."

"It's nothing," I say, although I know it needs stitches. Adela only let me go after I promised I would go to the hospital. But I can't go to a hospital today. I'll put a bandage on and go in the morning.

"Out, Gia," my voice rings out its final warning. I can't handle being near her for one more second.

She ignores me as her hands pull the buttons of my shirt apart. Her hands go to my wounds, and she carefully examines it.

"You were shot," she says calmly. Her eyes slowly moving back up from the wound to my eyes.

I don't answer her. She didn't question me anyway. She's

been around enough bullet wounds to know the answer without me explaining.

She sees whatever she is searching for in my eyes, and then she steps out of the tub brushing past me and disappearing out of the bathroom. Finally listening to my command.

It's what I wanted, but I'm left in the cold, empty bathroom by myself, and I suddenly wish she would have continued to disobey me. At least it would give me something to focus on.

"Sit," her voice rings through the bathroom as she places a first aid kit on the counter.

I sink onto the edge of the tub. I don't know why I listen to her. Probably because I have no fight left in me.

She opens the first aid kit and starts digging through it. She sighs and pulls a few items out of it.

"The hydrogen peroxide is expired, and there is nothing to stitch the wound closed. Let me clean it for you, and I think I can use these band-aids and gauze to at least stop the bleeding until Michi can get us some better supplies."

My eyes stay on her body, only a towel covering her naked body. Her hair is pulled up in a bun on top of her head, but a few curls hang down dripping water down onto her chest. The only part of her hair that got wet when she took a bath.

I don't say anything, and neither does she, as she kneels next to my body so she can examine the wound on my stomach. She pushes my shirt open, and I let it fall off my body.

She takes out the expired peroxide and some gauze.

"This is going to sting," she warns. Her big eyes fill with something I wasn't expecting to see. Kindness.

I don't move as she pours the liquid onto my wound. It doesn't sting. Maybe on another day, I would feel the burn, but not today. Today I'm too overwhelmed with my grief to feel something as minute as a tiny sting.

Gia bites her lip as she works. Her careful fingers work

quickly as she uses the band-aids like a stitch pulling my wound closed. She then takes the gauze and places it with a larger wrapping to protect the wound.

When she finishes, she sits back examining it, but I know she did a good job. The bleeding has slowed and will eventually stop. She did so well I may not even need stitches to keep the wound closed.

She doesn't ask me what happened. She doesn't ask how I ended up with a bullet wound.

And I don't ask how she knows how to heal a wound so well.

We both come from the same world. We know. We both deal with evil every day. We create it and harness it. I don't have to explain what happened. But the bullet isn't what is causing my despair. On any other day, I would be angry. I don't like having my life, or any of my employees' lives, threatened. But today, it was just a blip on the never-ending pain I feel.

I didn't even realize I had been shot until Adela pointed it out to me and made me promise I would go to the hospital. At least now that Gia has fixed me up I won't bleed to death tonight.

We both sit on the edge of the bath for a while, neither speaking or looking at each other. Occasionally she glances at me in the mirror out of the corner of her eye. She wants to say more. I can see it, but she knows I won't answer.

I can't answer even if I wanted to.

Slowly Gia stands. She licks her lips, turning to me with a wicked gleam in her eyes.

Any other day I would revel in that look. I would do almost anything to see it. But tonight it does nothing for me.

She drops the towel. I watch as it puddles on the floor.

She clears her throat, and my gaze travels upward over her thin legs that used to be scattered with heavy bruises. Now the bruises have lightened to the point of almost disappearing. The red cuts have turned to thin scars.

My eyes hover for a second over her pussy that appears to already be swollen and dripping. I don't allow my eyes to linger. If I had sex with her right now, I would destroy her. But as my eyes travel further up over her perky breasts and her red lips, I'm lost to my own darkness.

I couldn't get my revenge tonight, but I'm desperate to take it out on her. I can't drink the whiskey, but maybe if I drink her, I'll be able to forget. If only for a few minutes. Or I'll pass out afterward from the ecstasy.

"Use me," she says, her voice strong and determined.

Her words are exactly what I want to hear, but I know if I give in, I won't be able to hold back. I will ruin her. Destroy her. She will hate me more than she hates Dante.

"No." My voice rolls through the room bouncing off the walls. It took everything inside me to say it, and I don't have the strength to repeat it. But my voice tells her that. If she doesn't leave, I will demolish her.

She swallows hard, considering my unsaid words with every breath.

"I want to see your monster."

"Why?"

"Because I don't think you are one."

"Last chance." My voice is heavy with my final warning.

"Show me the darkest part of you. Show me the worst. Show me how bad you truly are."

She's testing me. Trying to release me, thinking if the worst part of me is out, then when my best returns, I'll let her go. It's a horrible plan because she won't survive the night.

I grab her smooth, slippery body and force her against the bathroom wall.

She gasps, her mouth wide and open as her head hits the wall roughly bouncing off.

I know it hurt, but the darkness doesn't care. I like the pain, the suffering, the agony. It matches my own and stops me from feeling alone.

"Your darkness doesn't scare me."

"It should."

I squeeze her neck tightly, watching the tiniest bit of panic in her eyes. But she doesn't struggle against me. She lets me suck the oxygen from her throat. I squeeze until she is on the verge of panicking. I've seen the look in her eyes before.

I saw it the first time she was with Dante. She didn't fight because it turned him on, but her eyes said she was defiant. She would survive.

She's wearing the same look now.

An idea forms in my head. A dark and dangerous one.

"Stand here and don't move." I turn and walk out of the bathroom, heading to my living room. I pull a security camera from a box I keep under the coffee table and carry it back to the bedroom. I flick the light on but don't actually turn it on. Gia won't know that though.

Then, I start gathering everything. A whip, rope, candles, and a knife. I lay them out on the bed so she will see them all when she enters. She wants the worst. She's about to get it.

"Come here, Gia."

My voice is loud and dominating, but I don't yell. And I know Gia will comply. She wants me to hurt her, so she can use it against me to get me to give her up later. She won't fight me tonight. She wants the worst.

I hear her careful footsteps against the tile and then she's standing in the doorway of the bedroom. Her eyes flicker to the bed and then to me.

Fear.

I see it in her eyes this time, but she blinks, and it's gone.

She takes deep breaths in and out, and I can't take my eyes off her breasts as they rise and fall.

I glance at the clock on the wall. Nine PM. Three hours until this day is over. And I plan on using every single one of them fucking Gia. She doesn't know it yet, but tonight will be the longest night of her life.

"You can't hide your fear, beautiful. I can see it in your eyes. Hear it in your breath. It oozes out of you."

"I'm not afraid of you."

I shake my head as I walk to her.

"Yes, you are."

"No."

I stop in front of her, watching as her breathing picks up speed, and she tries to anticipate my next move.

I touch her cheek letting my finger travel slowly down her neck. Goosebumps form over her arms. I love mixing calm with roughness. I like the extremes. I like being rough with a woman and seeing her limits.

In a split second, I change. I grab her body roughly and slam her to the bed. Her eyes close to keep in the pain. I expect her to tell me to stop at any point. I know she will last longer than this, for no reason other than her pride, but I know there will be more fear when she opens her eyes.

I walk slowly to the edge of the bed where I laid out my toys for tonight, so she could anticipate what is coming next, and her fear would intensify.

I grab the rope in my hand, feeling the threads, as I wait for her to open her eyes.

She does, and I get the most beautiful view into her soul. It's not fear I see. It's lust, and my darkness reflecting back at me. Being rough with her turned her on.

I smirk, knowing it won't last.

She eyes the rope in my hand, and she licks her lips slowly.

I grab her wrist and stretch her hand to the end of the bed, tying it to the bedpost. She tests the rope as I move to her second hand. It's only when both hands are tied up, does the panic start to creep in.

My lips lower to hers, and I kiss her roughly, enjoying her arms tied up, knowing she can't get free. At least, she thinks she can't get free. All she would have to say is one word, and I'd stop: "no." The second she says it this ends. I'm a monster, but not a rapist. I like hurting my victims by pushing them to their limit and not letting them know the rules.

When I pull back, her mouth lingers trying to kiss me further. I grab her ankle and tie it to the bedpost and then spread her other leg wide and tie it to the other bedpost.

She pants, both wanting me to come back and scared of what comes next, as she looks over at the items lying next to her. I take my time walking over to the dresser where I placed the camera.

I press the top, and the red light comes on, indicating the camera is on.

"I have clients tomorrow I owe a large debt to. They would love to see a video of my hot new slave."

I would never show your body to any man.

"I owe them for saving my life. They might cancel my debt if I share you with them."

I would never share you with anyone.

Her eyes flicker with every word.

"I don't believe you," she says, but her eyes focus in on the camera. She thinks she knows who I am, but she's never seen what turns me on. *What I crave more than anything.*

I walk toward her, my mind racing with all the horrendous things I want to do to her body. Whip her, bite her, suffocate her, cut her, fuck her. I want to mark her body. I want her to know she is mine. I want her to follow my every command. I want to know every inch of her body.

"You should," I say, grabbing the whip and hitting her smooth stomach with it.

She arches her back against the sharp pain, and she groans quietly, low in her throat. It's enough to make me hard in an instant and forget everything shitty about this day.

I strike her again, this time over her throbbing pussy. I get the reaction I need. A sharp cry followed by her body writhing against the rope keeping her body in position for me.

Normally, I would be able to be patient with her. Take my time to bring each strike. Take my time with each method of torturing her body. But today, I'm too worked up. I need to do everything to her body all at once. Afterward, I will take my time. My breathing has quickened, and my pulse is a venom shooting through my body with the need to own her body as no man has before.

She's going to hate me.

She raises her eyebrow like she knows I might back down. I might stop. We both want me to continue, just for entirely different reasons.

I can't stop. Not unless she says no.

"Please," she begs. It's not a plea to stop; it's a plea to continue.

I toss the whip on the floor after striking her body several more times, watching her perfect flesh turn pink in every place I hit her. And every time I'm rewarded with a cry, a groan, and, once, a tear. It hurts, but she doesn't tell me to stop.

I love her cries, it feeds the darkness, but when I climb up on the bed and find her thighs wet with her desire, I lose my fucking mind. She likes my darkness.

I can't wait to be inside her. So I grab her hips and take her all at once, my cock driving inside her.

She winces from the pain, but I don't give her time to rest. I fuck her hard as my mouth devours her breasts. I bite hard on her nipple.

And I know she would have slapped me if her hands were free. Her body jerks at the sharp pain.

"Want me to stop, princess?"

I lick her nipple, softening the pain before I strike again.

"Never," she whispers, but I'm not sure even she believes her own words.

I grin before biting down hard again. I move my mouth up, needing to leave a permanent mark with my teeth, branding her as mine. I bite down hard on the fleshy part of her breast.

"Fuck you, Conti!"

Just the reaction I was hoping for. My dick grows harder inside of her, reaching depths I haven't explored yet.

I've tied her up, beaten her, exposed her to other men, and bitten her. But it's not enough. She feels the pain. She's experienced what I'm capable of. But she's not been terrified.

I kiss her roughly, our tongues tangling and fighting with each other, telling me everything she is feeling. She's feeling a lot of emotions right now, but the main emotion she pushes through is determination. Don't stop.

Never.

The words she spoke earlier ring in my head. *Never is a long time.*

I grab the knife, the last of the toys for tonight. I bring it to her neck, and she freezes. The knife scares her. I knew it would. I've seen the fear in her eyes when Dante used it on her before.

I let her feel the cold metal against her neck. Let her know her life is in my hands. How easy it would be for me to kill her if I wanted to.

"You're so beautiful," I say, surprising us both with my compliment at this moment.

I swallow hard, needing to see her bleed.

She bites her lip, still holding her breath as she stares at me, realizing how big of a mistake she just made. I still my cock inside her.

"I want to make you bleed. I want you to know your body is mine to do as I please. And now that you've offered your body so willingly to me, you're mine, forever."

She sucks in a breath when I say forever, and I take the moment to scar her body. The knife pierces her skin at her neck, spilling red blood onto her glorious neck.

"Fuck!" she cries out as the pain hits her. I drive my cock inside her, hitting the glorious spot inside that will mark this moment not only with pain but pleasure.

My tongue laps over the cut, moving the blood over her neck while I continue to fuck her.

Tears trickle down her cheek, but she doesn't tell me to stop. She doesn't tell me to go to hell. She doesn't curse me at all.

She lets me fuck her.

I grab her neck, smearing the blood across her perfect skin as I do. I squeeze and watch the panic rise in her eyes as she can't catch her breath.

I fuck her harder, faster until she is mine completely. Mine to keep alive. Mine to make come. Mine to let die.

"Come, princess."

"I—"

"Come." I don't want to hear any words except her glorious screams as she comes.

I loosen my grip on her neck and dive my head down to kiss her and bring her back to life. She moans into my mouth taking my oxygen from me. And then she comes, screaming my fucking last name. The only name she knew to call me for all those weeks when Dante thought she was his. She was never his; she was always mine.

I shoot my cum into her tight cunt. Marking her again as *mine*. As soon as I finish, I take the knife and cut her arms and legs free.

And then I wait for the slap. I wait for the curse. I wait for the yelling.

Instead, she cries.

Shit.

I really did break her.

I run to the bathroom, grab a wet washcloth and some band-aids to heal her.

I sit carefully on the bed next to her as she cries more tears. Her hands are gripping her neck where blood still oozes.

I slowly push her hands down as I press the washcloth to her skin.

"I'm sorry. My monster is horrible. I'm sorry I hurt you. You should have told me to stop, and I would have."

Gia stops crying almost instantly. "You didn't hurt me."

I frown. "Your neck is bleeding. Your body is pink and red where I struck you. Your pussy is battered after how roughly I fucked you without making sure you were ready for me. I hurt you."

She pushes my hand down.

"No, you didn't. I thought you would. I was prepared for it. I thought after talking with Adela that I hated you. I just needed you to push me a little harder, and I would hate you forever. I knew you would push me far and rip me to pieces. I thought doing so would fill me with enough anger, all I would focus on going forward is the need to get my revenge on you."

I nod, understanding her need for revenge. I used her tonight to get my revenge.

"But I don't hate you."

"How? You must hate me." *I hate me.*

"What Adela told me about you, hurt. I thought I could

never forgive you, but just now I realized something. You were my guardian angel."

"Huh?"

"You watched me the entire time I was with Dante, didn't you?"

I suck in a breath, not liking where this is going.

"Didn't you?" she presses again.

"Yes, I watched you."

She smiles, and it's the most beautiful thing I've ever seen.

"You watched me and made sure I could survive. I don't know why you left me with him for as long as you did, but as soon as you realized I couldn't make it one more day, you got me out."

She takes a deep breath.

"Tonight, you repeated every horrible thing Dante did to me. But you didn't take anything from me. You didn't hurt me. You gave me my life back. You gave me my freedom. You let me choose the darkness. And you helped me replace the negative memories with something beautiful."

My mouth twitches, not agreeing or disagreeing with her.

"You made me stronger."

I look her up and down. I can't disagree with that. She looks stronger. Her eyes are clearer. Her body sits more upright. And when she smiles, she really smiles.

"And you made me fall in love with the darkness. I've been fighting it my entire life. But I've always been the princess of darkness. This is my home. And you gave me the power for that to be okay."

She leans forward and kisses me softly on the lips. "Thank you."

She pulls me to her and hugs me. Of all the ways I thought this was going to go, I never thought this was a possibility. I don't know what just happened, but I want it to happen again. I'm addicted to her body now.

"Again," she whispers into my ear before releasing me.

I grin. "You sure?"

She laughs. "No, but I want you. You excite and terrify me, and yet, I've never felt so free as when I'm with you."

I nod. I understand. I've only ever felt that way once, and then it was taken from me. I won't let Gia ever leave my side.

I still see the need for revenge in her eyes, but it's lessened a little. And when she looks at my body, I see the lust for more. She wants me, monster and all.

She thinks I didn't hurt her. I hope she's right. But I'm afraid I have, she just doesn't know it yet.

14

GIA

I'M SICK.

That's what last night made me realize. I'm one sick and twisted motherfucker. I loved what Caspian did to my body last night. I loved every mark, every scar, every sharp intake of pain.

I loved every kiss, every tease, and every thrust.

I loved it all.

I've never felt so free, and yet so trapped. I had a plan before. Find the hate and the need for revenge to free myself from him, but now, I can't live without our messed up sex.

I'm not sure I would ever come again with plain missionary sex. I want more.

I know yesterday was a bad day for Caspian. Something happened beyond just getting shot. He didn't tell me what, and honestly, it doesn't matter. He shared something much more precious with me. His true self.

He thought I would run afterward. He thought I would hate him. But now, I'm afraid I might love him.

I love his dark.

I love his light.

I need to find my place in this mess. Find a way to live in this world when I'm still consumed with a past that won't let me go. And the only way to truly stay with Caspian is if he grants me my freedom. Lets me choose whether I want to stay or go.

I don't know what I would choose if he gave me a choice at freedom right now. I want to explore Caspian more. See if he is the missing piece in my life. But I also want my revenge. I want to find my own way. I want to see my family.

"Good morning, beautiful," Caspian says, kissing me softly on the lips.

I smile and stretch; my body is completely sore from the twistedness of last night. This morning, the darkness is gone, and I see nothing but light in his eyes. Today he's Caspian, while last night he was Conti.

Conti is his darkness, while Caspian is the light. He may not realize it, but I love both parts of him. I couldn't take one without the other.

"Morning, Caspian."

"I'm Caspian again, huh?"

I nod. "Yes. Caspian is the person you are in front of most people. Conti, you reserve for the most intense situations."

"Which do you prefer?"

I shrug. "I like both parts of you."

He squeezes me, pulling me to him. It seems so normal. Something any couple would do in the morning after having sex all night. The difference is last night. It was the opposite of normal. But it was also everything I never knew I wanted.

"Come with me today."

I sit up, staring at him like he's just turned into an alien.

"What?" I ask even though I heard him perfectly well.

"Come with me to Rome. I have a client I have to meet with for a couple of days, so I have to go to Rome."

I half smile as I bite my lip, trying to keep my feelings under wrap. I don't want him to know I love what he is asking me. To go with him.

"Why?" I ask even though I know why. He doesn't want to be apart. And he's giving me a tiny bit of freedom. A reward for last night. No, maybe reward isn't the right word. Appreciation, maybe? Or he's claiming me as his.

"Because I'm selfish and don't want to be separated from you. I need you with me. Always."

Always.

I love that word.

God, I've got to stop saying, love. I don't love Caspian Conti. I don't even know him. And the parts I do know about him scare me.

I'm just infatuated with him. Especially after what happened last night.

There is still a part of me that is pissed at him for not saving me right away. I need to hold onto that part before I let the part that adores him consume me.

It's clear last night affected him the same way it did me.

"I'll go with you," I say. I want to ask him questions. I want to push this. I want to ask if this is the first step toward him granting me my freedom. But I don't.

It's enough for now. Soon, I will take my freedom, whether he grants it to me or not.

———

"I'm not playing a game with you," Caspian says for the hundredth time in the ten minutes we've been in the car.

I pout. "Why not? If you don't, I'm going to sing horribly along to the radio the entire time."

He frowns. "How about we sit quietly in the car on the way?"

"No, that's not fun. We always sit quietly. We never talk. We hardly know anything about each other."

"I know plenty about you."

I roll my eyes. "Only things you or Adela have looked up about me. Nothing directly from me."

I reach for the radio and turn it on. A Demi Lovato song comes on, and I start singing at the top of my lungs about having daddy issues. The irony is striking because I do have daddy issues.

Caspian turns the radio off, but I keep singing.

"Fine," he relents.

I grin from ear to ear. "So the rules are we get to take turns asking each other anything. And we have to answer each other's questions to get another turn."

"And if I don't want to answer?"

"Then, I win the game."

"And the winner gets?"

I've thought about this carefully. I could offer him something sexual, but he already knows I will do anything he wants without this silly game. I could ask for something worthy of playing, like my freedom, but then he wouldn't play or would just lie. I have nothing to offer him, but I know he's competitive. He hates losing. It's enough. I want this game to be light anyway. I'll only ask the tough questions when I want the game to be over.

"Bragging rights."

He narrows his eyes. "And how we will know if the other is telling the truth?"

"We will know." I have no doubt we will be able to tell.

"Okay, I'll go first. What is your favorite place in the world?"

"My house." He answers quickly. My first questions are meant to be light and easy so he will play along, but I didn't expect this answer.

"Seriously? You like your cabin? You're not talking about a bigger house you own somewhere else?"

"That seems like a second question."

I glare at him as his lips curl up. He's teasing me. I like it. I'm not used to this playful side of him.

"I'm talking about my only home. The house we share."

Share, that's a strange word to use when we don't share it. It's his; I'm just a captive there.

"Your turn."

"Why did you fall for a man like Roman?"

My mouth falls and my fingers, that were drumming along still to Demi Lovato in my head, still. I stare at him, and he stares back with the same intensity. He's not playing games with me. He won't ask any lighthearted questions. Only serious ones.

"Because I was desperate to be loved. I wanted an escape from the Carini family, and I couldn't do it on my own. Or at the time at least, I thought I couldn't. Roman paid attention to me. He offered me a chance at freedom, and I was stupid enough to think freedom was love."

Caspian stills for a second before he nods. "Your turn," he says as if I didn't just bare my heart to him.

"Why don't you buy expensive things? You make good money. Why don't you have a mansion?"

He raises an eyebrow as if he can't believe how easy my questions are, but this one I really want to know the answer to. "Because things mean nothing to me. I don't need a large house to relax at night."

"Then what do you spend your money on?"

He chuckles. "You don't know how to keep to your own rules, do you? That's a second question again. But if you must know, I spend it on Adela. I pay my employees more than fair to make sure they are loyal to me alone. And I use it to get my revenge."

I swallow hard at the word revenge. I know he needs revenge

the same as me. I don't know what happened to him, but I won't be asking him any questions about revenge today.

"Your turn."

"What do you want in life? What's your passion?"

"Jesus, you don't ask easy questions do you?"

He shrugs. "This is the easiest question I will ask. It should be easy for anyone who knows themselves at all."

I frown. "I don't know myself. That's my problem. I don't have a passion because I've never been allowed to be anything but a Carini."

"Do you like being a Carini?"

I smile smugly. "Now who isn't playing by the rules?"

He doesn't smile. He stares at me seriously waiting for me to answer. I guess it's only fair.

"Yes. I love being a Carini. There was once a time I hated it, but I think being a Carini made me stronger. It made me strong enough to survive these last few weeks. Without it, I would have dissolved into nothing."

He nods.

"My turn. Tell me about your first kiss."

He chuckles. "You know how to ask the tough questions," he says sarcastically.

I laugh and grab his hand. He lets me. This is normal. "First kiss was in the third grade on the playground with Luisa Pellegrini."

I smile, loving his normal answer. But my smile falters as I see the look in his eyes. He's about to ask me a question I won't want to answer. He's about to end the game. I can see it.

And then he smiles deviously. "Tell me who your favorite sexual partner was."

I laugh, blushing brightly, hating him for making me answer his question he already knows the answer to.

"This smug ass who doesn't deserve me, but managed to find

all the buttons to my body within seconds because he secretly crept on me for weeks."

"Hmm, he sounds pretty incredible. What's his name?"

"You, you fucktard."

His grin reaches his eyes. "Fucktard? That's a new one."

I try to pull my hand out of his, but he tightens his grip before kissing the back of my hand.

We continue on, asking silly questions back and forth, just trying to make each other laugh until we reach Rome.

Caspian gets us settled into our hotel room. The room is huge. He may not spend his money often, but he did tonight. I expect him to start talking to me about all the security he has installed before he leaves. I expect him to talk to me about the guards I'm sure he will have placed outside our door. Or the tracker he secretly placed inside my clothes when I was sleeping.

He doesn't.

Instead, he kisses me on the lips and says, "Come with me to my meeting."

I raise an eyebrow at him. "Why?"

He shrugs. "I want you by my side."

There is more he isn't telling me. But I won't get my answers unless I go. "Okay, I'll go with you. What should I wear?"

"Something that makes you feel powerful and strong."

His words have me worried I'm going to need all my strength to get through the meeting tonight.

But I do as he says. I change into a scarlet dress with plunging cleavage, while Caspian changes into a tuxedo.

His eyes never leave me as we dress, and mine never leave his. We both give promises of what we are going to do to each other when we return to the hotel room. But we keep our distance, or we will never leave the room in the first place. And as much as I want to stay in and let Caspian fuck me, I also want to leave. I want to enjoy a night with Caspian that isn't about **sex**, especially after our fun game in the car. I want a light, care-free night where I get more insight into his work.

"Ready, princess?" Caspian asks, holding out his arm to me as I finish applying red lipstick.

"As ready as I'll be when I don't know what we are doing or where we are going."

He stills, and I know he is considering telling me more, but then he changes his mind.

I grab his arm. "I promise it will be a pleasant surprise."

This has me even more intrigued, but I don't ask. I will find out soon enough.

Caspian leads me out of our hotel room, and to my surprise, no guards are sitting outside waiting for us to leave. We head down only one floor to where the hotel restaurant sits below our penthouse.

"Mr. Conti, your guest has already arrived. I'll show you to your table," the maître d' says.

Caspian leads me through the beautiful restaurant. At least I'll have a nice dinner in a gorgeous place.

Caspian leans down and whispers in my ear as we walk. "You want your freedom. After last night, I think I can give you a tiny piece of freedom. Revenge is freedom."

I don't understand what his words mean until we approach the table, arm in arm looking like the king and queen. I recognize the man at the table, and I realize immediately what Caspian is offering when he says I can get revenge.

Because sitting at the table is one of the men I hate most in the world.

Roman.

———

"Roman," I say, letting his name hang in the air.

Roman looks up at me. He recognized my voice, but he doesn't recognize the woman standing in front of him. I've been tortured, beaten, and raped. I should be weaker, but Caspian showed me how strong I am. And tonight, Roman is going to understand as well.

Caspian pulls out a chair, and I take a seat. Caspian takes his own seat.

"Gia, what a wonderful surprise to see you," Roman says, looking from me to Caspian. There is no fear in Roman's eyes, but there should be.

"I didn't realize you owned any women, Caspian," Roman says, using Caspian's first name instead of his last, like I've heard all of Caspian's other business associates address him.

"I don't," Caspian answers.

Caspian's answer shocks the hell out of me, but I don't let Roman know. *If Caspian doesn't own me, then what the hell are we doing?*

Roman chuckles. "Whatever you say. I'm glad you brought us some eye candy while we discuss our deal."

"I'm not eye candy," I say, glaring at Roman, trying to figure out how I'm going to kill him. Right now, cutting out his tongue so he can't speak to me like that is my first step.

"Really? Because that is what you look like to me," Roman says.

I don't wait for Caspian to give me any permission to start a fight with Roman. I can't wait.

I slam my heel into Roman's groin.

He cries out, like I just stabbed him, and grips his balls in pain.

I smirk. It feels good to cause him some pain. My eyes see Caspian out of the corner of my eye, looking at Roman like he's scum. I guess we won't be doing much eating after all.

Caspian gets up and grabs Roman's arm while he's still writhing in pain. He pulls him toward a back room while I follow. I'm not going to miss a second of Roman's pain.

When we get to the back room, Caspian slams the door shut behind us as he tosses Roman to the floor.

Roman takes his time getting up, still not realizing what danger he's in. It will make it all the better when I kill him.

"Our deal is off. I won't pay you anything to protect me when you let your whore disrespect me like that," Roman says.

"Gia didn't disrespect you," Caspian says, his eyes red.

I stomp toward Roman, knowing he could strangle me, snap my neck, or pull a gun on me before I realized what was happening, but I need to be close to him to say what I need to say.

"I am not a whore," I say, kicking Roman again.

He cries out but doesn't fight back. *Why doesn't he fight back?*

I glance behind me and see Caspian has a gun pointed at Roman. I smirk. This is where Caspian and I understand each other the most. In the darkness.

"I am not yours. I never was. You didn't own me. You didn't have the ability to sell me."

I kick him again and again after each sentence, needing to get my frustration and anger out on him. He lets me and takes each punch and kick with a grunt or a groan. I watch as the blood slowly pours down his face.

"You are a fucking coward. A weak, shithole that didn't have the balls to hurt me yourself. So you sold me. You sold me and pretended it was just a business transaction. That it didn't bother you what happened to me next.

"Well, guess what? I was raped. I was beaten until I couldn't move. I was violated until sex became torture. My life was threatened every day because of you."

He cowers on the floor beneath me, curling up into himself.

"You are nothing to me. Fucking nothing!"

I take a deep breath, trying to get oxygen in my body as I keep yelling.

"You think you won. You got your money. You sold me, and I was no longer your problem. I told you I would come after you. I said you would pay for what you did. Today is that day.

"You think I'm weaker because of what you did, but I'm stronger. I'm your fucking nightmare."

I kick him again, watching the blood spill from his eyes where my heel clipped him.

My body shakes with anger. I thought I wanted to torture Roman, make him suffer for hours or days, but he isn't worth my time. I want him gone.

Caspian steps forward when I've finished all I need to say.

I think Caspian is going to shoot Roman. Eliminate him. Wipe him from my nightmares with one bullet.

Instead, Caspian thrusts the cold metal into my hand. I stare at the gun for a second. I don't know if Caspian realizes how dark I am. The things that I have done in my past. He calls me princess, but I'm not a princess. I'm just as evil and twisted as him.

Roman won't be my first kill. Not by a long shot. But I will remember this kill forever.

Caspian steps back, knowing I don't need him by my side to do what has to be done. Roman needs to be killed, if for no other reason than to protect other women from the same fate.

But that's not why I'm killing him though. I kill him for me.

"Goodbye, Roman."

I pull the trigger and watch the blood spill. The light in his eyes leaves, and then he's nothing.

I watch him a second longer before I walk back to Caspian and hold out the gun to him.

"Keep it," he says.

I don't question him. I put the gun in the back of my dress and underwear. And then I kiss Caspian with everything I have. I've never needed a kiss so much in my life. This kiss is everything I've ever needed. I need it more than air.

My stomach grumbles, and Caspian pulls away. "I should feed you."

I smirk. "No, you should fuck me."

15

CASPIAN

Gia Carini is a badass.

That's all I can think about as I carry the sexiest woman I've ever met back to our hotel room. Her heels are digging into my side. Heels that she used to kick that son of a bitch in the balls.

It was amazing to watch. I always knew she was strong and fucking incredible. But I never realized just how fucking badass until now. I know Gia's brothers didn't let her get too involved in the business side of things. They wanted to protect her and for good reason. So I doubted she would kill Roman when I handed her my gun.

I knew she was angry. I knew she needed revenge, but I thought if she found the strength to pull the trigger, she'd miss and I'd have to finish the bastard.

She aimed right for his heart and killed him without a second thought. She's more like me than I could have ever imagined.

She was just dark and dangerous, but earlier in the car she was the sweetest, funniest woman. And that makes her even sexier. One moment she could live out my fantasies, and the next she could kill me. Especially since I let her keep the gun.

She won't use the gun to kill me. I know her well enough to know that. Her feelings for me are too strong. She's not pissed at me like the others, even though I'm just as much of the reason she is in this mess as Roman or Dante is. I've hurt her the same. So if she does decide to use the gun against me, I deserve it.

But she needs the gun for her protection. Now that I know she is capable of proficiently using a gun, I trust her with it. She could kill an intruder as easily as I could. And it will make her feel better protected now that she is starting to make enemies.

I've planted the story that Roman stole her back. He was the one that stole her from Dante. Dante will be looking for her with a greater intensity now. And I'll be the one to find her. She will want to help me.

I can't focus on Dante now. Now I have the sexiest, most incredible, amazing, awesome, badass woman in the world. And I plan on making good use of her wanting me while I have the chance.

We burst through the door of the hotel room I sprung for. I never buy anything this expensive, not anymore. I only told a half-truth when I told Gia why I don't have anything nice or expensive. I don't find much use in more expensive things, it's true, but I also don't feel worthy.

I got this hotel room for Gia. She's worthy of a penthouse. She's worthy of a lot more.

Her hands claw at my neck, desperate to put the adrenaline and high she is feeling to use. And she wants to use me.

"Slow down, princess," I say as she kisses my neck and starts undoing my tie.

"Why?" she purrs.

"Because I want to savor you."

"You can as long as it's dark and dirty, as fucking messed up as it was last night."

Last night was incredible. The best night of my life by far when it should have been my worst. I've never gone that far with a woman before. No woman has ever been able or willing to take on the sadistic side of me. The controlling asshole that lives in the dark.

But she craved it, same as me. And now she wants more.

"Be careful what you wish for, beautiful."

She grins. "I want everything. All of your darkness. I want to feel it all."

Her words are what I've wanted to hear all this time. I've needed to hear them for so long, but no woman has ever measured to her. Now the woman of my fantasies finally exists. She's real.

She rips my tie off. "I want to know all the darkest parts of your soul."

I smile. "You already do."

She cocks her head to the side and whispers in my ear. "You haven't found my darkest places yet. So find them."

Damn, my cock is hard.

I'm the one who is going to need to fucking slow down. I'm still holding her in my arms, and we both grow wild at the same time. She rips off my tie, and I kiss down her neck, hungrily until I reach her cleavage, which is far too exposed in this dress for going in public. I want her to myself. I don't want to share, even a glimpse of her.

My tie is off, my shirt is unbuttoned, and my cock strains against my zipper about to burst through my pants. I remove the gun from the back of her dress, toss it to the nightstand, and let our bodies fall to the bed. I don't have any of the dark toys I had before to play with her, but that doesn't mean this session is going to be light. I don't know how to go back into the light with her.

Her nails dig into my chest, and I know that she is still in the dark with me. If I don't tie her up, she's going to be just as rough with me as I am with her. I welcome it.

Last time, I needed control. This time, I need her with me.

I grab her dress and rip it down the middle, the sparkly sequins scattering to the bed as I rip.

She glares at me. "I loved this dress. Why did you ruin it?"

"Because you can't wear it in public anymore now. I can't stand to see other guys looking at you in it."

She blushes. I think she's going to scold me. "Are you jealous, Caspian?"

"No, jealous would imply you look at other men in a room. You don't. I'm infuriated with any man that looks at what's mine."

Her eyes darken, her breath catches, and her nipples stand at attention waiting for me. My caveman words turn her on, instead of turning her off.

"Fuck me, Caspian," she says, growing impatient with our pause.

I grab her legs and pull her cunt to me so I can taste the sweet pleasure I know is dripping there. My tongue darts inside her, and her body sings.

"God!" she moans, unable to even say my name, as I make her body wiggle beneath me.

I smirk, pushing my tongue deeper inside her and bringing her right to the brink. She wants to come so badly, but she also wants what comes next.

I push her, moving my tongue deeper inside her body as I hit the sweet spot that will make her do anything I want.

She explodes around my tongue.

"Yes, Conti!"

Her screams still me. She's called me Conti several times before, and every time she does, it reminds me of someone else.

And it melts my cold heart. This time it shatters the ice holding it together until there is nothing left.

I sit up abruptly, not believing what I'm doing.

"Conti?" Gia sits up slowly, feeling the coldness in the room. The chill that won't go away until I start talking.

I feel tears burning my eyes. Tears I haven't cried in almost five years.

"I should have saved you."

Gia shivers as she wraps the ripped dress around her body.

"You did save me."

"No, I should have saved you the second you fell into my lap."

"You couldn't. Dante would have killed you."

"No, I could have saved you. It would have ruined my relationship with Dante, sure, but I could have prevented every horrible thing from happening to you, and I didn't because I was selfish."

Gia scoots closer to me but doesn't touch me as we both sit half naked on the edge of the oversized king bed. I never expected to spill my heart to a woman again, but here I am, ripping my own heart to shreds. Gia doesn't say anything. She waits until I can speak again.

"I needed revenge more than I wanted to save you. You shouldn't want to fuck me. I'm a bigger monster than Dante and Roman combined."

She nods. "I know you could have saved me. I know you were torn and wanted to. Adela told me. At that moment, I hated you, but I knew you had to have a reason for not saving me. And last night I realized you were watching over me, making sure I never got hurt so badly I couldn't recover. You saved me the second you could."

"No!" I grab Gia's face as tears stream down my face. "I let that disgusting excuse of a man hurt you. I let him touch you. I let him rape you, and I did nothing. There is no excuse good enough to let you go through that."

Tears burn her eyes, but she doesn't let them fall. "Just tell me why."

"I had the perfect wife—"

She gasps when I say, wife. And then she realizes she shouldn't act surprised and relaxes.

"I had the perfect wife. She was beautiful, smart, determined. She was a nurse. She devoted her life to helping kids that didn't have any money to pay her. She only took enough money to feed and clothe herself. She was a saint."

The tears will never stop now that I've started.

"She was my light. She kept me pure. She knew there was a darkness inside me, but she kept the darkness at bay."

"She sounds wonderful."

"She was. She was heavenly. Purer than an angel. She saved me, helped me find my purpose in providing security systems to protect the innocent from the evil."

I can't look at Gia as I talk about my wife. It's too much. So I stare at my hands. Hands that have done so much wrong.

"But security isn't pure. I got mixed into a world of evil. I tried to stay away, but it sucked me in like a vacuum I could get free of.

"We'd been married two years when she was taken in the middle of the night. My security system had failed us...failed her. Yesterday was the anniversary of her being taken."

I roar out my anger needing the pain to go away. I've been numb for too long to be able to handle this pain now.

"I searched every day for her for a year. One year I searched. I found her, but it was too late. She was dead and gone, tossed out like trash. I brought her back to my home in the woods and buried her in the garden, but it wasn't enough. I needed to get her revenge."

Gia nods but keeps her hands in her lap, even though I can tell she wants to comfort me, she knows I won't accept it right now.

"Dante Russo was the one who took her. I vowed the day I found her, I would torture and kill him the way he did her. I needed the best security system to get a way in. I needed a system he would want. So I became the best. And then I needed something Dante would truly mourn when I stole it."

"Me," Gia says.

I nod.

"I'm not valuable to him. I'm just a body he can fuck. He doesn't care about me any more than he does any other woman."

I shake my head. "I planned to install the system, watch him, and find his weakness. But the second I saw you run out of the car, I knew it was you. You would become his weakness because you instantly became mine."

She sucks in a breath.

"I've watched him every day since I took you. He's gone mad. He would do anything to get you back. And now that I've tortured him with your disappearance, can I kill him."

Gia takes a second to herself and then grabs my cheeks, wiping my tears with her thumbs. "I forgive you."

More tears fall. Of all the things she could say now, I never expected her to say that.

"You can't forgive me."

She smiles carefully. "I just did. You don't get to tell me how I feel. I forgive you. I can't understand what you've been through. I've never lost someone like that, but I've experienced pain and if there were something I could do to make that pain lessen for someone I love, then I would. Even if it meant hurting someone else."

I grab her neck and kiss her firmly on the lips, sucking all the air from her.

"How can you be this perfect?" I ask against her lips.

She kisses me again, needing our lips together. "I'm no more perfect than you are. We are just kindred spirits, both searching for the same thing. Revenge."

I devour her lips now. I need to be inside her as quickly as possible. She needs the same thing. Her hands are at the waistband of my pants, trying to push them off.

I rip her panties down and push inside her without waiting to see if she is ready for me or not. From her wince, her body wasn't prepared, but her moans and clawing on my back tell me she doesn't care. Her soul can't wait.

I rock in and out of her, gripping her tightly as I fuck her. But I'm not just fucking her. There is something different happening, but I can't find the word to describe it. Because no word can describe the connection between us. No matter what happens next, it's unbreakable.

"What was her name?" Gia asks, and that's when I realize what's happening. This is for my wife. For a connection I had with a woman that was stolen from me too soon. A woman I never deserved. Whatever beautiful connection is happening now is because of her.

"Clara Conti."

Gia pauses for a second, honoring her, and then she kisses me hard on the lips. And I fuck her like tomorrow might never come. And it might not.

I don't know how this ends with Gia and me. How am I going to give her up? Because I can't keep her.

16

GIA

Caspian told me his darkest secret, but I can never tell him mine. I forgave him. He would never forgive me.

Everything has changed since I killed Roman. We've been home a week, and it's almost like we are a normal couple. We don't talk about me leaving, or giving me my freedom anymore. I already have my freedom. I got it the day he tracked down Roman for me to kill and then let me keep the gun. Any time I want to use it to leave, I could.

But I don't want to leave.

Caspian's home is becoming my home. His desires are becoming mine. We both want the same thing.

Revenge on Dante Russo.

We want him to hurt as much as possible, and then when he's done hurting, we want to kill him.

We don't talk about it. Instead, we talk about normal things. The weather, food, drinks, our day. But it's always on our minds. Even when we are fucking.

Our desire for revenge is too strong for anything else. And I'm tired of not talking about it. Once it's done, then we can focus on what the hell we are doing together. What our future could hold. Until it's over, we are trapped in our revenge.

At one point revenge was my freedom, but now I'm afraid it's starting to hold me back.

Caspian is sitting outside on his computer. He usually sits there after dinner, soaking in the last drops of sunlight on his computer. I usually sit next to him reading a book. But today, I helped Michi clean up the dishes first. So when I finally join Caspian outside, the sun has all but set.

"You ready to go inside?" he asks when I join him.

"No."

He glances up from his computer, sensing the trepidation in my voice.

"When are we going to kill Dante?" I ask. I know he has a plan, he just hasn't shared it with me yet.

He closes his computer, and I'm afraid he's closing our conversation.

"Soon, but I'm not sure I can bring you with me, or if I do if I can let you kill him. I've been planning this for five years. I need to be the one to kill him. I can't just hand you the gun like I did with Roman."

It hurts that I won't be the one to kill him, but as long as he's dead, it doesn't matter. "I understand."

He narrows his eyes. "How could you? My wife was taken from me, but you were the one who went through so much. And I let it happen."

I grab his face and kiss him softly, annoyed even though I've forgiven him, he still hasn't forgiven himself.

"Stop. I understand. I didn't die. I didn't lose anything. You did."

He turns away, not able to look at me. I hate it when he does this. Shuts me out. I know he doesn't owe me anything. We aren't in a real relationship. I don't even know what "we" are. But it still hurts.

He turns back. "Take your revenge out on me."

I frown. "No, I forgive you. I don't want to hurt you."

His thumb strokes my cheek before he pulls me onto his lap. "I need you to. I can't forgive myself. My nightmares are no longer about Clara. They are about you. Every night I have a nightmare about what Dante did to you. I hate myself for letting him lay a hand on you, much less hurt you every night. I can't live with myself. Take out your revenge on me."

I search his eyes and find him near breaking. He needs this. And when I search my heart, I realize I do too. I may have forgiven him, but it still hurts. I need to let the pain go. And this might be how.

"Okay."

He lifts me and sets me down on my feet. Then he gathers his computer and empty wine glass and walks inside. I follow after, both terrified and exhilarated with what is about to happen.

He sets the computer and glass down on the counter where Michi is still cleaning.

Caspian looks at Michi, and he knows. Michi really needs his own place if Caspian is going to keep kicking him out. Michi heads out without a word.

Then, Caspian walks to the bedroom. My feet can barely move, but I make it somehow. Must be muscle memory that moves me.

I stand in the doorway and watch as Caspian gathers items. Whips, chains, floggers, knives, anything destructive he can find. He lays them all out on the bed. And then he starts undressing. Removing his shirt slowly, then his pants, until he's standing in nothing but his underwear. He considers his next move for a second and then he removes his boxers too. It's not sexual. He's baring his all to me.

And I've never seen a stronger man.

"Please," he whispers, and I know what he's asking. Please make the pain go away, for both of us.

Then he lies down on the bed and waits.

I take a couple of deep breaths, letting go of the compassion I have for Caspian and let the hate I've pushed away back in.

He could have saved me but didn't.

I repeat those words over and over until I'm lost in them. Then I stomp toward the chains, knowing I have to tie him up. No matter how much he says he wants this, as soon as the first crack of pain hits him, he will try to stop me. For this to work, he has to be completely vulnerable.

So I pick up the metal cuffs and loop one around the post and then attach the cuff to his wrist. He looks at me with sad eyes but doesn't say anything. He just watches. I feel the fear oozing off of him, but know it has nothing to do with the pain he's about to feel. It has everything to do with us. Where will we be when this is over?

I walk to his other arm and attach it to the bed, doing the same to his legs.

"Try to break free," I command.

He pulls hard with his arms and legs, but he can't move.

I nod and then close my eyes. Filling everything in me with the memories of Dante. Him striking me, beating me, raping me. His cock driving into me is what does it the most. So I focus on the image. Of what it felt like to have a cock push into me when I'm dry and unwilling. The burn, the violation, the pain. I let it consume me, and then I open my eyes.

I don't see Caspian lying on the bed; I see Dante.

I grab the first item I can find. A bat. I bring it high over my head and then I beat down on the broken body in front of me.

"I fucking hate you!" I scream as I hit the body hard in the stomach. I can't see anything but rage.

I lift the bat and strike again and again. I'm rewarded with a loud groan each time, but it's not enough. I want the screams I let out every time Dante hurt me.

I strike his chest one more time with the bat before I move onto the whip.

I don't know if it will hurt more or less, but I plan on using every instrument I can until I hear the screams.

I'm not as skilled with the whip, so my first attempt misses, hitting the bed. But my second strike hits my target's legs. His legs jump at the sting, leaving bright red welts.

It's not enough.

I've formed the bruises on him with the bat. I've formed the redness with the whip. I need the scars. I need the cries.

The cock inside me was one of the worst. The absolute worst. I don't want to fuck this man. He doesn't deserve a second of my pleasure. But the next worst thing was the sharpness of the blade. Knowing he could take my life if he wanted with a slip of the knife.

I grab the sharp blade, and then I climb onto Dante's body. I straddle his hard chest as I hold the knife to his neck as he has to me so many times before.

"Do it. I deserve it," he says.

I freeze the knife over his artery. He does deserve it. He deserves to die.

I shove the knife hard against his neck until I see blood. But I still don't hear screams. I need his screams! I need to know I hurt him as badly as he hurt me.

I remove the knife from his neck and aim for his heart, stabbing his chest.

He screams. It's high pitched and terrifying, and it feeds my soul. I want more.

I stab him again. He's going to get a slow torturous death.

"I'm so sorry, Gia. I'm so sorry. I deserve this."

His voice makes me stop. That isn't the voice of Dante.

I stop the knife and close my eyes, trying to push the hate back down. When I open again, I see Caspian on the bed. Bleeding to death.

"No! Oh my god! What did I do?"

I jump off of him, dropping the knife and race to get the first aid kit.

When I climb back on the bed, his breathing has slowed, and his eyes have grown heavy.

"Shh, you did nothing wrong. You did what had to be done. And if I die, it's what needs to happen," Caspian says.

I pull out gauze, covering the wound to attempt to stop the bleeding.

"Don't talk like that. You aren't going to die."

But I'm not sure. There is a lot of blood. I don't think I hit his heart, but I hit something major.

"Michi!" I yell, hoping he's in the house or nearby. I get no answer.

I glance at the handcuffs I used to restrain him. I need the key to release him. He's going to die restrained to his bed if I don't help him.

Fuck.

But if I worry about releasing him, he will definitely die.

I dig through the first aid kit while I keep applying pressure with my other hand. I find the stapler and drugs I requested Michi stock after the last time Caspian was injured. I don't have time for morphine though.

"It's going to be okay," I say calmly. I take out the stapler.

"Look away," I tell him. He turns his head and bites his lip knowing more pain is coming. I staple the wound over and over. Each time the pain ripping into his heart. Each time I pray he doesn't die because of me. *What was I thinking? I have no control over my demons.*

"One more," I say as the last staple goes in.

I press the gauze back, and the bleeding has reduced greatly.

I exhale deeply. He's going to be okay. He needs a hospital, but he's going to survive.

"I'm so sorry," I say.

I look at him, but he doesn't respond.

"Caspian?"

Nothing.

I lower my head over his chest. He isn't breathing.

Shit.

I blow into his mouth and start doing compressions.

"Please, Caspian!"

I keep compressing over his heart, praying his staples don't pop open and the bleeding doesn't start all over again.

"Don't you dare die, Caspian!"

More compressions, but he's not breathing.

"You are going to be an uncle. You hear me! You can't die!"

More compressions.

"I need your help to kill Dante. Clara can't be avenged without your help."

Two breaths.

"I love you. Please don't leave me."

More compressions.

Then, coughing.

"Caspian!" He's alive.

I ease off him, letting him get some good breaths in.

"Thank god, you're alive," I cry. Tears are streaming down my face. "I've never been so scared in my life."

"Liar," Caspian teases.

More tears. "I can't believe you let me do that. What were

you thinking? I could have killed you! You should have stopped me."

"I couldn't exactly stop you with the cuffs. And I would have deserved it."

"No! You don't deserve to die."

He tries to comfort me but can't because he's still tied up, but I can't leave him for a second right now to grab the key from the bathroom.

So I lay my head on the uninjured side of his chest. I need to get Michi to help me get him to a hospital soon, but right now I can't move him.

"I'm so sorry," I whisper as tears stream from my eyes to his chest.

"You have nothing to be sorry for; you saved me."

"No, I didn't. I almost killed you."

"No, you killed Dante. You killed the pain in me for what I let happen to you. You let go of your own trauma. And now, we can survive so much stronger. We helped each other heal."

I nod, not believing he is comforting me right now after I just killed him.

"I almost let you die; you almost killed me. I saved you; you saved me. I think we are even now. We can move forward and decide our future without anything holding us back."

I know his words are true. And I wish he was right. That we are even now. But we aren't even close to even. He might have been selfish, but everything he did was for Clara Conti, a woman who deserved his love. I may love Caspian Conti, but I don't deserve to be loved in return. I don't know if he heard any of my words when he was out. I hope he didn't because I don't want him to love me in return.

He may have hurt me, but I'm the real monster.

17

CASPIAN

GIA ALMOST KILLED ME. Sometimes I wish she had. Then the pain would finally be gone.

She has taken care of me these last few weeks. Life has been normal. My wounds have healed, and we don't talk about that night at all. We don't talk about Dante or the pain we caused each other.

All we do is heal, together. It's taken time, but we are finally healed. At least as healed as we can be.

But we can't continue like this.

"We need to talk," I say to Gia. She's sitting next to me on her patio chair reading. The last time we talked out here, it ended in her stabbing me. This time, I hope it ends better. But I'm still dreading the conversation I'm about to have because it's the beginning of the end.

She looks up from her book, her eyes big. "Maybe we should go somewhere else to talk first. The last time we talked out here, it didn't end well."

She kisses me softly on the cheek. "What's up?" she says more calmly.

"I have a plan to kill Dante."

She folds her book and puts it on the end table before turning her feet to the side to give me her full attention.

"When?"

"Next week."

She nods then smiles. "Good, I can't wait to have him out of our lives for good."

"I need your help though."

Her smile brightens. "Anything."

"I want to fake your death. That will make him suffer the most. You may not realize he loves you, but he does."

"He does not love me."

"Not in the typical sense. He loves owning you. He loves hurting you. He would hate if anyone else were the one to break you."

She thinks for a moment. "Okay, I'll do it."

I suck in a breath I've been holding. I want to fake her death not only to make him suffer but also because it will keep her safe if my plan fails. He can't come searching for her if she's dead.

"And next week after I kill him, you can finally be free."

Her body freezes at the word *free*.

I give her time to recover, not pushing her to understand what she's feeling in her head.

"What do you mean by *free*?"

"I mean you can leave. Go home to your family. Start your new life away from here."

She nods slowly, like she can't believe the words she's hearing. She stares at the ground for the longest time, before staring back up at me.

"I love you, Caspian."

Fuck.

My worst nightmare happened. She can't love me. I will

break her when she finds out I'm incapable of love. Clara took my heart with her when she died. I haven't loved since. I can't.

"When I kill Dante next week, I will have Michi pack your things and make sure you are on a plane to see your brothers in the US."

I stand up, needing to be done with this conversation. If I stay and talk, it will only make this worse.

"Seriously? That's all I get. I tell you I love you and you leave? This can't be happening!"

"I told you I would hurt you. I don't love you. In one week, you should go."

Her face drops like I just told her her puppy died or something else horrendous. All I did was tell her I didn't love her.

"No. I'm not leaving. You love me too you big jerk, even if you won't say it now. You wouldn't have saved me if you didn't care about me. You wouldn't have let me hurt you if you didn't love me. You wouldn't do everything to protect me if you didn't love me. You love me!"

I stand firm. "I'm incapable of love, Gia. Even you. I'm sorry. I know I said you would never be free, but I meant that figuratively, not literally. You will never be free of your past."

"You love me."

I grab her body and jerk her to me. "No, I don't. I never can. I'm sorry for being nice to you. For saving you. I knew I would hurt you. I was afraid you would fall in love with me, but I couldn't stop it and keep you. I'm selfish, but then you already know that. I used you to get what I wanted from Dante. That's it."

The last part stings the worst. I can see the devastation in her eyes. The drop in her body. The loss in her face. I hurt her worse than Dante ever did, and it kills me. But this is for the best. This must end. If she stays in my life, she will end up dead. And she deserves a man who can love her like she needs to be loved. Not constantly saved by a selfish asshole like me.

Gia looks at me for one more moment with tears in her eyes. But she doesn't let them fall. I've watched her many nights in Dante's room where she was able to hold back her tears, despite the pain she was in. She's had plenty of practice holding her tears in.

I want her to stay, to fight because I don't want to lose her, but I need to let her go.

She makes the right decision. She walks out the door. Most likely to sulk in the bedroom or in Michi's room.

I give her a minute before I head inside and grab a bottle of whiskey and then head back outside. I'll drink myself into oblivion and pass out on the couch. I'll be doing a lot of that in the near future.

I may not love her, but it won't stop me from missing her. I'm not good at missing people. I'm destructive and cruel. But after Dante's dead, it won't matter because I'll have nothing left to live for.

————

Gia's gone.

The words float around in my head but don't really land. She's not gone. She can't be.

But she will be soon, and when she is, I don't know what to do with myself. I'm not sure I will survive without her in my life. I've grown used to her light-heartedness. Her beauty. Her smart mouth.

I will miss her too much.

"Caspian!" my body falls off the chair and lands with a thud. *Damn it, that's going to leave a bruise in the morning.*

I open my eyes and see Adela standing over me, but there appears to be four of her.

"What?" I snap, annoyed she brought me out of my sleep. When I'm asleep, I don't have to remember Gia is leaving me in less than a week.

"Gia's gone," Adela says.

"No, she's not. She's in my bedroom."

"Caspian, she's gone."

I shake my head as I sit up carefully, trying to not puke.

"She ran out. She looked upset. Did you fight?"

I nod. It was close enough to a fight.

Adela's body shakes, and she finally has my attention. "Where is she? Who followed her?"

"I'm so sorry, Caspian. I was on duty. But I've had an upset stomach all day, and I stepped away from the feed for a few minutes. You were with her; I thought she was safe."

"Adela, what happened?" My heart freezes as I already know what happened.

"Da—" She doesn't get the word out. I know. Dante took her.

I jump up and race inside, grabbing my gun and running to my car with Adela on my heels. I don't know how Dante found out she was here, but he did. And I will do anything to get her back.

"Caspian stop! You're drunk! Let me drive," Adela yells.

"Get in the car. I've never been more sober in my life."

Adela frowns but jumps in the passenger seat. She starts calling in any member of the team she can get ahold of to help us as I drive to Dante's place.

Gia ran out because of me, and now she's his. I can't lose her. I can't lose another woman I love.

Love.

Shit, I love her. I didn't think it was possible, but now that she's gone, I'm lost forever.

18

———

GIA

MY ARMS ARE TIED behind my back as the light tickles into my eyes again. I don't have to open my eyes fully to know where I am. I can smell the rotten flesh, taste the blood, and feel the cold floor beneath me.

Dante stole me, again.

And now I'm back in the same room of his house; I swore I would never return. But this time, I will escape after I kill Dante.

The door opens, and I feel Dante's presence before I see him. He smells of sweat and blood and fear.

I stare at him as he walks in without a word, and I've never seen his face redder. His nostrils flare wide, and his teeth grind together, striding toward me.

I won't cower in the corner though, no matter how much my head hurts.

I stand slowly, even though my hands are tied behind my back, I'm ready for a fight. He will not touch me again.

Dante chuckles, watching me. "You think you are going to be able to stop me?"

"Yes, I will. And by the time I leave here, you will be dead. If not by my hand, then by Caspian's."

He smirks. "Oh yes, Caspian. The man who stole you. I thought he stole you because he wanted you as his slave. But you look very well taken care of."

I frown. I don't want Dante talking about Caspian.

Dante walks closer to me, and I stand tall, ready to fight as best I can if he touches me.

"I have a feeling we will be meeting your new lover sooner rather than later. He won't like that I get to touch you, not now that he's had you. He will realize what a good prize you are."

"I'm not a prize. I'm a person."

Dante shrugs. "No, you are mine." His hand clenches tightly around my arm, and I wince at the touch. Before a touch like that wouldn't have affected me, but now it's all I can think about. The pain shoots through me, making me realize how weak I am compared to him. If Dante wants to rape me, there isn't much I can do to prevent it.

"And this time, when I'm finished with you, I will kill you before any man has a chance to take you again."

I shiver at his words. He's wrong. He will be dead long before me.

The door slams open, and Caspian stands in the doorway. His gun is drawn, and it's pointed at Dante. I knew Caspian would come for me. He hurt me worse than Dante ever thought about hurting me, but he will do anything to protect me, even if he doesn't love me.

Dante chuckles. "Nice of you to finally show up. I thought you were supposedly the best at security, but I was able to snatch her up with ease. It took you hours to even realize she was gone. I almost thought you weren't coming, which would have been tragic, because then I would have had to hunt you down and kill you for taking what's mine."

"Let her go, Dante. Then we can work this out man to man," Caspian says, his eyes searching me for signs of any trauma.

I'm fine, I mouth to him.

His shoulders relax when he realizes my words are true. Dante, on the other hand, hasn't loosened his grip on my arm. I can't move. And I don't know how good of a shot Caspian is. Can he shoot Dante while missing me?

"You seem to be missing your partner though. Where is she?" Dante says.

"I'm here alone," Caspian answers, and my eyes widen. I don't want Adela here, but I'm not sure Caspian can take Dante and his men out on his own.

Dante chuckles. "You're a terrible liar, Caspian."

My heart stills at Dante's words.

Dante's phone buzzes, and he pulls it from his pocket casually, not acting like his life is currently in danger.

"Do you have her?" Dante asks.

There's a pause.

"Good," Dante says ending the call. "It appears my guards have your sister. They are under strict instructions to kill her within three minutes if you don't arrive to save her. My insurance that I remain alive."

Caspian's eyes widen in fear. Sweat drips down his face as he tries to decide if Dante is lying or not. He can't risk Dante not lying though.

"You're lying," Caspian says, and my heart stops. He can't choose me over Adela. He has to save her first.

"Stay here, and we will find out," Dante says.

"Adela's pregnant," I whisper through tears. She can't die. She has a husband who loves her. She has a baby on the way. She has a future. She deserves to be happy and live.

"Please, save her," I continue. I don't add first. I doubt there will be time to save us both.

Caspian swallows down tears I see in his eyes. He looks at me, and then Dante, and then back to me. His eyes tell me he will be back, soon. And then he disappears before either of us have a chance to change our minds.

"Now that he is taken care of, where were we?" Dante asks.

"Your guards won't kill Caspian. He'll fight them off. He'll save Adela. And then he will be back to kill you. So I suggest you spend your time running as far away as you can."

He turns me toward him, his disgusting cock pushing against my stomach.

"I hired new men. I have faith they will be able to handle Caspian. You should have said your goodbyes."

Dante's cocky as he says his words, but he's never been more wrong. He doesn't know how Caspian feels. He doesn't realize Caspian needs his revenge for killing his wife.

I struggle against the rope tying my arms together as Dante smirks, his slimy hands groping my body.

Please hurry back, Caspian.

No, I need to find a way out of this. I can.

"You're nothing but a coward. You always have been. I'm surprised you don't have four men in here holding me down like before. You can't even rape me like a man."

Dante's eyes are searing into mine. "You want a fair fight?"

"Yes."

His grin widens. "Then, let's fight."

He pulls out his knife, and I close my eyes afraid he's going to stab me. Instead, my arms pull free of the rope.

I'm in so much shock I don't anticipate the kick to my ribs. It knocks me over, and I hit the wall before sliding to the ground.

"It doesn't matter if you are tied up or not. I'm stronger than you, slave. I will win. I will rape you. And then, I will kill you. Submit now, and I will make sure your death is painless."

His words drive me, just like before. I want revenge and here is my chance to take it.

I'm stronger than Dante. Not physically, but mentally. I'm a survivor. I'm scrappy. And I know more about his world than he realizes.

He kicks me again, and my body recoils.

Think.

I need a solution. A way out.

I need a weapon. He's still holding the knife. I won't be able to snatch it from his hand. But I bet he has a gun.

And there is only one place a guy like him would keep a gun. In the waistband of his pants where he can access it quickly.

Stand, I command myself.

I do.

Dante kicks me again, but I don't let him knock me down no matter how much pain I'm in. As I stand, he grabs me, forcing my arms down to my sides.

I frown as I try to wiggle out of his grasp. His mouth comes down on mine, slobbering roughly over my mouth.

"You're mine, bitch. Don't forget it."

He tosses me down on the bed and jumps on top of me. I freeze. My mind goes to my happy place with Caspian, as my survival mechanism sets in.

No.

Focus on the gun.

He grabs my shirt and starts ripping it open as his mouth comes down on my body. It takes everything in me to not fight him off. To let his mouth take my nipple in his mouth. I need him close to me and not holding my arms down, so I can reach his gun.

I move my hands slowly, trying not to draw attention to them being free as Dante bites down hard and making me tear up.

But I can't wait. I won't let him rape me.

I grab for the waistband, find the metal gun, and shoot him in the leg.

Dante curses as he falls off of me. I scoot my body out from under him and stand to point the gun at him. Dante holds his hands up as he writhes in pain.

"You don't have the balls to kill me," Dante says.

I smirk. He doesn't know I was the one who killed Roman. That I would kill him in a second without thinking if I didn't think Caspian needed this more.

Caspian may not love me, but I love him. And we need to know that Adela is safe before we kill Dante. We may need him to get her back.

"You don't think I will kill you?"

"No."

I shake my head, tightening my grip on the gun. "If you move an inch, I will shoot you."

"I don't think you will."

He moves, and I shoot him in the other leg.

"Fuck you, bitch!"

I grin. "I'm not a liar. I will kill you if you move. I've killed plenty of men before. And even if I hadn't, the things you did to me would have made me strong enough to kill you in an instant. The only reason you are continuing to breathe is that Caspian needs to kill you more than I do."

Dante laughs. "You aren't strong enough."

"Gia's plenty strong enough. Adela's safe. Kill him, Gia," Caspian says as he enters the room.

His words should be enough for me to pull the trigger, but I can't do that. Caspian needs this more than me. He's needed this for five years.

I lower the gun and hold it out to Caspian. "You need this more."

Caspian holds onto the gun and then tries to push it back into my hands, but I won't let him.

"I love you. Let this be my final gift." I give him the gun, and then I step back. I may not get to kill Dante, but I can watch the white leave his eyes.

Caspian lifts the gun and aims it at Dante, and for the first time, I see fear in Dante's eyes.

"You took Clara from me. You deserve to be tortured over and over for the pain you caused her. You stole her, tortured her, raped her, and then killed her. But I'm a compassionate person. I will kill you swiftly if you apologize for what you did."

Dante shakes his head. "I never stole a Clara."

Caspian's finger tightens around the trigger. "You took her from me five years ago. And then threw her out with the trash like she was nothing. You were about to do the same thing to Gia and hundreds of other women. You remember her."

"I don't because she doesn't exist."

I can see Caspian's rage grow as Dante admits he doesn't remember Clara. Caspian has a lot of control, but he doesn't have much control left.

"Admit what you did, you fucking cunt."

Caspian's hand shakes as he stares at Dante with all the pain he's felt for years.

Dante turns from Caspian and looks at me with his lust-filled disgusting eyes.

I jump as the bullet leaves Caspian's gun without warning. It hits Dante in the head, and he falls to the ground, dead in an instant.

Caspian runs to me and throws his arms around me, both of us shaking.

"Did he hurt you?" Caspian's voice trembles as he speaks and looks me over.

I close the shirt he ripped around my body. "He barely touched me before I snatched his gun."

Caspian exhales. "You promise?"

I nod.

"Thank you for coming back and saving me."

"I didn't save you; you saved yourself."

I smile weakly.

"Is Adela okay?"

He nods. "Yes, she's shaken up, but she's fine. She will be popping a baby out in six months without a problem."

I smile. "You knew."

He nods. "I knew, but it still killed me to leave you here not knowing if you were going to live or die."

"You made the right decision. I wouldn't have forgiven you if you had saved me and anything had happened to Adela."

"I know. It still killed me."

Tears fill my eyes. I won't let him see me cry over him again.

"I'm going to go call my brothers. I'm sure they are worried sick. They will send a plane to get me."

Caspian steps in front of me, stopping me from leaving.

"Your brothers know where you are. They've known the entire time I've had you."

"What?"

"They trusted I would keep you safe. If you were with them, you would have jeopardized their lives, and it would have been one of the first places Dante would have looked."

"I should still talk to them, now that he's gone."

"Stop. Stop running."

I freeze.

"I'm sorry. For everything, but most importantly for breaking your heart. And for not telling you I love you too."

"What?"

Caspian grabs me and kisses me with everything he has. He dips me, holding me in his arms as he deepens the kiss, his tongue tasting every drop inside my mouth.

When he pulls back, I see the love in his eyes. He loves me, and I love him. This should be our happily ever after. Our perfect ending, but it isn't. I can't start our lives together on a lie. He has to know my darkest secret. Only then, can he decide if he loves me.

"There is a reason Dante didn't admit to killing Clara."

Caspian steps back, he can sense what I'm going to say.

"Dante may have stolen her, but he sold her to my family. To my father."

Caspian takes another step back, and I can feel him slipping further away from me.

"Your father? Enrico Carini?"

I nod. "He was the one who raped her. He broke her."

"He killed her?"

I swallow, trying to keep the words from leaving my mouth, but he has to hear them. He has to know the truth.

"No, I killed her."

19

CASPIAN

GIA COULDN'T HAVE KILLED Clara. It's not possible. Gia has to be lying or misunderstanding what happened. I know Gia's past is dark, but she couldn't have killed an innocent woman.

"No," I say.

Tears stream down her pink cheeks. Whatever happened, I can forgive Gia. I love her. I almost lost her to Dante again. I won't let her go again.

I force my legs forward toward her to show my support. She needs to know there is nothing she can say to make me leave her.

"I remember Clara. She was a beautiful, strong, innocent woman. She loved life, but my father broke her almost instantly. She was so fragile, so naïve that it was easy for him to break her.

"I thought I could help her. So one night after father had gone to bed, I snuck into her room. I couldn't sneak her out; her body was too broken to run. And I couldn't lift her on my own. But I could bring her a weapon. I couldn't kill my father myself, but she could. She just needed the gun.

"So I provided her one. But she was too far gone to keep fighting. She just wanted the pain to end."

She doesn't continue, instead, her voice cracks. Clara used the gun to end her life and her suffering. I don't blame Clara for what she did. I couldn't rescue her, and she didn't grow up in the world that Gia did. Clara didn't have the same fight that Gia has.

Rage and pain hit me again. And I have nothing and no one to take it out on.

"I need revenge."

"Enrico is gone. He's already dead."

I turn, needing to find something to take out my anger on.

She races in front of me. "Take it out on me. I deserve it. I never should have given her the gun in her condition."

I look away. I can't look at her. It hurts too much.

She grabs my face and turns me toward her. "Take out your revenge on me."

"I can't. The last time we did, one of us almost died."

She wipes her tears. "It's worth the risk if it means I have a shot at keeping you."

She's right. It's worth the risk.

She smiles weakly at me and then walks to the bed and lies down offering her body to me.

This room is filled with the darkest of items. Items I could use to destroy her. But it's not what I want.

I want rough. I want fast. And I want to know if we can find love in the dark. Or if we are meant to wander this world apart.

I grab her body and rip her pants until she is naked.

She moans as I do, but this isn't about pleasure. This is about releasing my rage.

I flip her over and find her sweet ass. I spank her hard, watching as her flesh turns red. She cries out, but it just sparks my deeper rage.

I hate her for what she did.

I'm not sure I can forgive her.

I'm not sure if I can forgive myself.

Or if the love I felt a minute ago was even really love or just worry.

I spank her again and again, watching the pain spread as I undo my pants. I need to be inside her whether she is ready for me or not. I need to fuck her ass and show her how much pain I'm in.

I push my pants down, and then I push my hard cock against her asshole, and in one movement, I thrust in. She screams in pain but doesn't try to stop me.

I want to do worse. More spanking. Slam into her body harder. Grab instruments to mark her body.

I settle for slamming hard into her while I slap her ass.

"Conti!" she cries out.

I still. *What am I doing?*

My rage immediately disappears as she moans my name. She sacrificed herself to save my sister. She's sacrificing her body now for a chance at love. And I'm repaying her by hurting her after I've already done more than enough horrible things to hurt her.

I pull out and flip her over before thrusting my cock back into her.

"I'm so sorry, princess," I say kissing her lips as hard as I can. Tears sting both of our eyes as we kiss harder. Gia wraps her arms around my neck as I slowly rock in and out.

"I love you," I whisper against her lips. "I'm so sorry. I'll never screw up again."

Gia smiles. "You will, and I'll forgive you. Just like I'll screw up as well. I love you."

I smile. I don't think I'll ever stop smiling as long as I have her. But right now I need to focus. I have the love of my life to make love to, and I want to rock her world.

She bites her lip as she sees my expression change. "I want to love you forever, Gia."

"I'll never stop loving you, Conti."

I laugh. "But I might stop if you keep calling me by my dad's name."

She laughs too, but her laughs quickly change to moans as I take her perky nipple into my mouth and rock against her clit. I know exactly how to play her body. It doesn't matter we are in the darkest place, where Gia was raped and with the dead body of her rapist a few feet away. We won't remember any of that after tonight. Because tonight we are reclaiming it as ours.

I never thought I could love again after Clara. Clara was my light, and Gia brings out my dark. I thought I needed to stay firmly in the light, but Gia has taught me that it's okay to live in the darkness. Because even in the darkness, there is light. And together we can always find our way back out through our love.

EPILOGUE

GIA

"I HAVE SOME EXCITING NEWS," I say into the phone where my sisters-in-law Nina and Eden are on the line.

"Oh my god, you're engaged!" Nina shouts.

"No."

"You're pregnant!" Eden says.

I laugh. "No."

I can hear the audible sadness in both Nina and Eden's voices.

"Don't worry, Caspian and I are still going strong, I just don't think either of us is ready to settle down and have kids." I don't add that I don't think we will want kids ever. Our lives are too dangerous to add kids to.

"So what's the exciting news?" Eden asks.

"I've finally found my passion! I'm officially a partner with Caspian and Adela in the security business. We install security systems in the worst of the worst homes and businesses, and then use that information to turn them over to the police or to kill them."

Silence.

I knew my news wouldn't go over well, but finally, I get a

response. "That's amazing!" I hear them both say at the same time.

"Really, it's amazing! I'm so proud of you. You are really going to make a difference. You are such a badass. You have the skills, and you know this world so well," Nina says.

"Thank you."

"Just wait a little until you tell your brothers. They won't take the news well. They will probably try to ring Caspian's neck for letting you do such a dangerous job, but you are going to do amazingly well."

I smile. "I'll wait until we come to your house Christmas to tell them."

I hear a baby crying in the background. "We need to go. Be safe and visit soon. We all miss you." The line is disconnected as the cries get louder in the background.

I smile. I miss them too.

Caspian comes into the living room carrying a plate of sandwiches. "How did it go?" he asks even though I know he heard every word of our conversation. The cons of living in such a small home. The pros far outweigh the cons though. I love being so close to Caspian all the time. This house feels cozy, like a real home, instead of the coldness of the mansion my family used to call home.

"Well, my sisters think it's a great idea."

Caspian raises his eyebrows. "And your brothers?"

"We agreed it was best to wait to tell them."

Caspian laughs. "Good, that means I can live another day."

I curl up next to him on the couch and snatch a sandwich off his plate.

"I love our life. And I love you for letting me risk my life, same as you."

"It's hard. Maybe one day it will get easier. But I can't stop you from being the badass, warrior you are."

I kiss him on the lips, smiling widely. I can't get enough of him.

"I overheard your sisters-in-law though. Do you want to get married and have kids? Have the typical life?"

"No. I don't have a need to get married. I already know I'm going to spend the rest of my life with you without a piece of paper telling me so. And kids, our lives are too dangerous to bring kids into the mix. All I need is you."

"I feel the same way." He rubs his nose against mine.

And I lean into the crook of his arm while I chomp down on my sandwich.

Arlo and Nina travel to stay safe from the dangers our family has put us in. They never stay in one place for long, and that keeps them safe.

Matteo and Eden use the distance of the US and Eden's job as a prosecutor to keep them safe.

But Caspian and I confront the darkness head-on. Our lives are the riskiest, but it's worth it to live the life we want.

Italy is my home, and I would never leave it. As for my childhood home I love, and for Clive and Erick, the remaining men on my revenge list, maybe one day I'll face them and get my home back. As for now, I've realized I don't need revenge to be happy or free. Love already set me free.

The End

Thank you so much for reading! The Carinis' story isn't over yet! The final chapter is Dirty Epilogue, an extended epilogue that features all of the Carinis. It will be available for FREE later this month here→www.ellamiles.com/dirtyepilogue/

If you loved the Dirty series, keep reading to get a sneak peek of my romantic suspense The Maybe Series...

THE MAYBE SERIES — CHAPTER ONE

"Hey, boring," my loudmouthed friend says, bouncing into my apartment. Scarlett didn't bother to knock. She just opened the door like she lives here. She practically does though.

We've known each other our entire lives. If it weren't for our parents' pocketbooks allowing each of us to have our own luxury apartment, we would have been roommates. Sometimes, I wish we had been anyway, so we could have gotten the real college experience. It would have never worked though. Our clothes alone would have been too much to fit into one apartment together.

"Hey, Scar," I say, not looking up from the book I'm using to study for my art history exam.

Scarlett plops down next to me on the white sectional. She stretches out until she is covering half of the couch. "Really? It's our last weekend before we graduate. Why the hell are you studying?"

"Because we have finals next week."

"So what? It's Friday night. Study on Monday morning, like the rest of us."

I shake my head as I turn the page. "I want to get good grades, unlike the rest of you."

Scarlett reaches over and pulls the book from my lap. She tosses it onto the floor before I can even protest.

I exhale, looking at Scarlett. "What are you doing here? I thought you were going out dancing with Jake tonight."

I watch as she flips her long ombre brown-colored locks over her shoulder before she begins picking the polish off her perfectly manicured hands.

"I broke up with Jake," she says, not looking up at me.

"Ugh, not again."

She quickly sits up. "Don't lecture me, she who has never had a boyfriend."

I roll my eyes. "I've had a boyfriend before. There is just no point in dating right now. I'm supposed to be focusing on my studies and modeling jobs."

Scarlett yawns. "Boring."

"How did this become about me? You're the one who broke up with that boy again. That makes it the fifth time this year."

"I'm tired of being tied down. I want to be single when I go off into the world."

I get up and go pick up my textbook off the floor. "But why are you here? You still have time to find a date to take you out tonight." I turn to face her. "Or you could go alone since that's what you want so much."

She smiles mischievously at me. "Or you could go with me?"

"No," I say as I settle back into the couch.

When I glance back up, she pouts her lip, and her eyes grow sad in a way only she knows how to do.

"Please," she begs.

I can't help the smile that grows over my lips from seeing her beg like this. She's not begging because she needs someone to go out to the bars with her. Scarlett is the most confident person I know. She loves being the center of attention. She's asking because she wants me to have fun for once in my life.

"I don't know...maybe," I say, giving her the same answer I've told her hundreds of times before.

"Come on, Kins. You don't need to study. You have the highest grades in our class, and you don't even like theater."

"I do, too," I protest even though I don't, not really. I suck at acting. I find the history behind theater interesting, but I have no interest in really working in that field.

On autopilot, I pull my phone out of my pocket. I begin texting my dad, like I always do. But I know what he's going to say before I even ask. He'll say no. It's seven thirty. I'm supposed to call him in an hour for our weekly updates. I love his calls, but I think he chose Friday nights just to keep me out of the bars and clubs, not that I mind. It's also why he chose Yale for me over some of the other colleges. Yale isn't exactly known for being a party school. I prefer his calls to drinking until I puke, like Scarlett does.

My thumb hesitates over the phone. I've never really had the opportunity to try out my theory on drinking until I puke. I've just assumed I would prefer talking with my father to it. And I can't make any more mistakes.

I move my thumb to press Send when Scarlett's body tackles me to the ground. My phone drops from my hand and slides across the hardwood floor. It's a miracle it doesn't shatter, but from where I lie on the ground with Scarlett's body pressed to me, it doesn't seem like it even got a scratch on it.

"What—get off of me, Scar." I try to wiggle out from underneath her bony body, but it's no use. I have no leverage to get out from underneath her.

I stop fighting and resolve to listen to her. "What was that for?"

"I am *not* letting you ask your father for permission to go to a bar tonight."

I narrow my eyes at her, trying to figure out if I can use the element of surprise to get out from under her grasp. "Why not?"

"Because you are a grown-ass woman who can make her own decisions. You turned twenty-one three days ago, and you haven't even so much as gone out for a drink yet."

I frown. "I did, too, go out for a drink."

"Yeah, you had champagne with your family, and you were back by nine o'clock. That's not exactly what I mean, Kins."

"It was a weeknight! What was I supposed to do? Go out and get so drunk that I wouldn't have even made it to my classes the next morning?"

Scarlett nods. "Yeah, that's exactly what you were supposed to do. That's what any normal college student would have done."

I shake my head. "But we aren't normal."

"Yeah, well, for one night, we are going to be."

"No, I'm going to study, and then I'm going to call my dad in an hour, like I always do."

I reach back for my phone that is just a foot or so above my head, but Scarlett pins my arms to the ground with her hands.

"Come on, Scar, let me go," I whine.

I try my best to give her puppy-dog eyes, like she did with me earlier, but I'm not the best actress in the world. And even if I were, Scarlett doesn't have a heart. She's ruthless when she's made up her mind.

"Not going to work." Scarlett's grip on my arms tightens. "The way I see it, you have two options. One, you can spend the night lying on the floor with me sitting on you. Or two, you can get your scrawny ass into that closet of yours, pick out something slutty to wear, and go out clubbing with me."

I wear a pinched expression as I stare up in annoyance at my supposed friend who is blackmailing me into going out. I look at my scrawny arms. I knew I should have gone to the gym at least once or twice. I don't have an ounce of muscle on my body to fight her off.

"You're really going to sit on me all night if I don't agree to your terms?"

She smiles. "All night."

"Fine." I sigh. "I'll go with you. Just let me text my dad to let him know."

"Nope." Scarlett jumps off of me and scoops my phone up. She turns the phone off before slipping it into her cleavage. "You are not asking your daddy for permission. Tonight, you're going to have fun."

I quickly stand up before Scarlett changes her mind and pushes me back to the ground.

"Let's go then." If I appease Scarlett and go to a bar for an hour or so, then I will still have enough time to come back, call my dad, and get some studying in before bed. No harm done.

Scarlett laughs. "Oh, Kins, you know nobody goes out this early. Plus, we need time to change if we are going to find a guy for me to hook up with tonight."

She grabs my hand, and I follow her past my kitchen where my favorite chocolate-colored chandelier hangs overhead. Then, we go down my hallway to the spare bedroom that I turned into a closet—or boutique is more like it. The room is overflowing with clothes I was given from various designers after doing shoots for them. The other half of the room is filled with every brand of makeup and every jewelry and accessory that I have ever worn. It is every girl's dream. I'm just not sure it's my dream.

Scarlett begins scrolling through the clothes in my closet, as easily as she would if it were hers. She is attracted to the tight skirts and cleavage tops that will show off her bought curves. She begins stripping before trying on a variety of my clothes, and then she throws them onto the floor after deciding they aren't sexy enough.

I sigh. I'll have a mess to clean up tonight. Unlike Scarlett, I don't have a maid to clean up after me. It's not that I can't afford one. I just like my own space. I don't want someone coming into my home, touching my things.

I head to the other end of my closet, toward the clothes I just got after the last shoot I did. I find the black crop top that I was given. I take my simple white T-shirt off and replace it with the black crop top. I leave my dark skinny jeans on but replace my flats with a pair of black high heels.

I take a seat at the table in front of a large mirror where I begin to touch up my makeup. My long blonde hair is already curled as it hangs down my back. I apply some red lipstick to finish my look before I look at myself. I'm happy with what is staring back in the mirror until Scarlett stands behind me.

We are both models and both beautiful in our own right. But while I model for *Seventeen* magazine, Scarlett models for Victoria's Secret. I look seventeen, and she looks twenty-five. Guys find me attractive, but guys want to sleep with her.

It's for the best that guys never want to sleep with me. I shouldn't date anyway, not when my father and grandfather are the ones who will be choosing who I marry.

"All right, I'm ready." Scarlett glances at herself in the mirror one more time. "Let's go."

I grab a silver clutch, and I throw some cash and my ID into it. "Can I get my phone back now?"

Scarlett smiles. "Maybe."

I roll my eyes.

I have a terrible feeling about tonight. I shouldn't be doing this. My father is going to be pissed when I don't call him tonight. *But what's the worst that can happen?* I'll get drunk and end up puking on Scarlett's couch. My father will yell at me tomorrow for the first time in five years. Then, everyone will get over it. It's not like one mistake can ruin your life.

Except, I think as I pause at the open door of my apartment, *one mistake can.*

I shake my head. That was five years ago. This is nothing like that. This time, it won't be a mistake.

Keep reading The Maybe Series Here!

FREE BOOKS

<u>EllaMiles.com/freebooks</u>

Want to get my full length romance *Not Sorry* for **free**?

Want to get my **free** bonus novella—*Aligned: Ever After?*

Want to know when I put my books on sale for **free or 99 cents**?

You can get all of the above and more goodies here:
EllaMiles.com/freebooks

ABOUT THE AUTHOR

Ella Miles writes steamy romance with a twist. She's currently living her own happily ever after near the Rocky Mountains with her high school sweetheart husband. Her heart is also taken by her goofy four year old black lab that is scared of everything, including her own shadow.

Ella is a USA Today Bestselling author, author of the Amazon top 100 bestselling books: TOO MUCH and SAVAGE LOVE. She is also the author of the ALIGNED series, MAYBE series, DEFINITELY series, UNFORGIVABLE series, NOT SORRY, and DIRTY series.

Stalk me at:
www.ellamiles.com
ella@ellamiles.com

9 781951 114107